Tales from
2020

K.N. SALUSTRO

ISBN-13: 978-1-7370670-0-9

Also by K.N. Salustro

The Star Hunters:
Chasing Shadows
Unbroken Light
Light Runner

The Arkin Races

Cause of Death: ???

DEDICATION

For Ben, except for the one with the cat.
That one's for Aunt Karen.

Author's Note

2020.

Truly a year of infamy. So many things happened, a lot of them terrible, a lot of them bizarre, and, weird as it seems, there were some good things in there, too. It's the year that either marks when everything changed forever, or it's the year that a lot of us are going to squint back on, turn to each other, and say, "Did that actually happen?"

For a lot of people, that year will be both.

I could start rambling here about what 2020 meant for me, but frankly, I don't really want to. On the back cover, I promised you escapism, and that is what I'm going to give you. If you want to get right to it, you have my blessing to skip ahead and get to the fiction. I don't mind, really. But if you want some context for everything you're about to read…

I wrote these stories while doing research for my next novel, in the hopes of keeping my writing sharp while I flooded my head with facts about pirates and old ships. I also wrote them whenever I needed to get out of my own head for a bit. Some were cathartic, some were personal challenges, and some were just a little silly. It depended on what I needed at the time.

Of the seven stories, three started out as a string of plot points from a roll of Rory's Story Cubes. Three more were written in response to contest prompts. And one just crept into the room while I was attending my first ever funeral over Zoom. Oddly enough, that's not the saddest one.

Catharsis is weird for me, and my writing doesn't like to come from pain.

Instead, "Fire in the Sky" came from a Story Cubes roll, just a random drop of the picture dice. I recorded me figuring out that story with the intent to share it to YouTube, as with the others Story Cubes videos I've made, but that day, I had to keep my voice down out of courtesy for my sleeping partner, and then the thunderstorm wound up making that a moot point, anyway. All said, it wasn't a great video, so it disappeared into the depths of Things You Will Never See. But I did end up with an odd little creation story of sorts that kept sticking in my head until I finally put it down on paper.

"The Thunderbird" began as a contest entry, where we had to thread a connection between a photo of a pristine blue mountain lake with another photo of a dark highway running off into a thunderstorm. I took that hard into fantasy, and wound up with a story that didn't place, but that I liked enough to keep working on. Several rewrites later, we have a tale of monster killers.

Pivoting right over to something completely different, "The Beetle and the Twins" is probably the most fun I've had writing a short story in a long time. It started out as a Story Cubes roll and has remained pretty faithful to its original plot, although with a few new layers added in. It's ridiculous, and I love it.

"The Marvel Artist" is another Story Cubes originator, and one that gave me a bit of trouble throughout the writing process. I kept getting caught between writing a character I wanted to loathe, and one that I wanted to sympathize with. He ended up being both, although he may fall more firmly on the loathe side for you. Who knows? (You will, once you read it, and I'll only know if you leave a review. (Please do that. Reviews are helpful. Seriously.)) For me, he hits that streak of arrogance that slithers through all young artists who have come to understand that hey, they're actually good at this, and they could be great. Artists aren't "supposed" to show you that streak. We're "supposed" to be modest and indulge in our own self-loathing and let our work speak for itself while we brood in the corner and pretend that it didn't take a lot of hard work and self-motivation to make the thing. We don't actually like doing that. It takes us all a different amount of time to realize that, and some of us never really do, or we go skidding down the slope of extremism and get real pretentious about everything. It takes a lot of time and work to get to the point where you can balance your pride in your art with the humility needed to keep learning and improving. But sometimes, you just want to snap the paintbrush and go sulk.

"Don't Look Back" is another pivot into something completely different, and my first attempt at writing anything that could be remotely considered horror. I still mostly consider it fantasy. This story started as a response to an October contest prompt where we had to write a scary story with the words "don't turn around" included. I didn't finish it in time to submit, but I liked it enough to keep it around on my computer. After a while, I dusted it off and gave it some revisions, and now I maybe wonder if my pollen allergies are starting to influence my stories a bit. You'll see what I mean.

"Grandmother's Familiar" is the story that snuck up during the Zoom funeral. The funeral was not for a grandmother (both of mine passed a good long while ago), but it was for someone who was a fixture in my early life, and she is and will continue to be deeply, sorely missed. This is probably the closest I come to writing fueled by pain. But I added a bratty animal to give the character (and I guess myself) a lifeline as she sorts through loss experienced at a distance, and memories that don't quite measure up to reality. Past that, everything else in there is pure fiction, except for that claustrophobic little mountain town. That's based off of where I grew up.

Finally, "How Not to Make Cookies in Space" started out as another didn't-finish-in-time contest response to the prompt, "Write a holiday-themed story that includes the phrase, 'That's not how you make cookies!'" But as with the others, I liked it enough to keep it, and that means this collection gets to end on a sweet note. Pun intended.

So, as promised, there's no plague fiction here, just some stories that helped me escape reality when I needed to. Maybe they'll do the same for you.

Thank you, and enjoy.

- K.

Contents

Fire in the Sky

At the beginning of time, there was a fire.

It was born into a dark, violent world, back when the stars could hurl their wrath across space and the sun did not care if its planets lived or died. Alone and afraid, the fire fled as far as it could, jumping across the scorched lands under the indifferent eyes of the stars. It burned hot and bright, bringing light to the dark and sense to the void, slowly learning to take comfort in its own presence. Its world may have been cruel and unforgiving, but where the fire was, there was warmth and brightness, and for a long, long while, that was enough.

But as time spun out and aged everything it touched, the fire began to share its world with forces too unlike itself.

The rain came first, dousing much of the fire and hurting it and chasing it away from the deep basins that began to fill with the first waters of the seas. The fire let the rains have those territories. It was darker down there, and harder to burn, and it preferred the surface anyway.

Life came next, green and supple. At first, the fire tried to burn alongside this new growth, but it found the life resistant to its warmth. The fire burned hotter, trying to comfort the new life carving out a hold on this dark world. It burned too hot. The life screamed and died beneath the fire's touch. The fire held on, trying to right what had gone so horribly wrong, until there was only ash on the ground. The rain came to see what the commotion was about, and only found a dead stretch of land.

The seas filled and the air changed and the winds came, and the fire burned on. It thought that it found a playmate in the winds, which whipped its flames to new heights and carried the fire farther and faster than it had ever gone before, but the wind would vanish as quickly as it would come, leaving the fire alone and in strange places it did not recognize anymore. Places that were choked with life and would attract the attention of the rains if the fire lingered too long. So the fire took what it needed to in order to survive, and fled before the rain could find and kill it.

As survival became the rule of existence, the world's surface became less and less familiar to the fire. Things were coming out of the sea and taking unsteady steps on the beaches. The world was rich with tough, green things that the fire could not easily burn. And the rain was falling so hard and so fast now, spreading itself everywhere. The fire was terrified, and retreated to the only safe haven left: the center of the world.

It was dark below the surface, and even more unforgiving than the days when the stars had sent rocks smashing into the planet, but it was safe from the other elements down there. So, the fire took shelter in the place where no one would ever see its brilliant colors or bask in its warmth or share in its light, but at least the fire could survive.

Time matured the world. As the planet left its youth behind, so too did it let the knowledge of the hidden fire fall away. Knowledge became history, which became stories, became legends, became memories, which faded until the fire was forgotten.

Until someone let it out.

Time had turned the world old by then. Life had grown complacent, and allowed some of its green to wither and die. The rain had grown tired, and wandered over the seas, taking steadily fading joy in the deep blues that could only be found away from the land. The rain avoided the land a lot in those days, ever since the peak of the two-legged things that had consumed the world and then tried to abandon it when their prime had passed. The rain did not care much for them and the things they did, so the rain left them to their strange goals and only stirred up storms when the two-legged things came over the water in floating vessels. It followed, then, that the rain did not immediately notice when the two-legged things broke into the world, and chased the fire out of its hiding place.

Terrified that the others had finally come to kill it, the fire erupted out of the world and spread as far and as wide as it could. Everywhere it went, the fire found a world decayed and dying, and the things that had resisted it before burned all too easily beneath its touch, becoming char and ash on the wind. The fire slowed a little, trying to understand what had happened to the surface in the time it had spent beneath the world. Comprehension eluded it, and the fire grew angry. This was not how the world was supposed to be. Before the fire had left, everything had been alive and growing. Terrifying for the fire, yes, but firmly there. This pliant surface that disintegrated at the slightest touch of flame? The fire did not know what to do with this. So it did the only thing it understood.

It burned.

The fire burned far and wide, consuming everything in its path. It spread its warmth and light as far as it could reach. It left black ash in its wake, leeching the color from the world until there were only its own fearsome reds to bathe the earth and the sky. When the fire reached the shoreline, it bellowed a challenge over the waters, promising to boil the seas if the rain did not come and stop it. Its call went unanswered, so the fire burned and burned, until there was nothing left but ash.

Alone and gasping for breath, the fire curled up on the last bit of land that could sustain it. Its reach had dwindled to a few flames, and its color was a flickering orange instead of that wild wall of unstoppable red. It looked around and mourned for the world that was. The world that had never been kind to the fire and chased it underground, but had still been beautiful. The fire looked up at the sky, searching for the stars that had watched it so indifferently before. They had not changed much. Some of them were gone, and some of them were new, and many of them had moved across the sky, but one important thing remained the same: they were cold and distant and cared not what happened to the fire.

The fire cried one final challenge at them, sending its flame as high as it could, before it collapsed into embers.

The rain came then, soft and silent and ashamed. It knew that it had been away for too long, and that it had allowed the world to fall apart. It washed the ash into the sea, angrily at first, then more and more gently as it realized that there was nothing beneath the ash that the fire could have hurt. There was nothing left.

When the rain found the spot where the fire had finally died, in a pool of white ash among all the gray and black, the rain mourned. The colors were gone from the world, and the rain was dark and silent and lonely without them. So the rain flooded the land until it, too, was spent. The last thing it left behind was a small, glittering arc of color that dissipated in air that could no longer sustain it, but the rain threw everything it had left into that last rainbow, and the world flashed one final time with the blues and greens of life, and the reds and yellows of the fire that had come before and after everything.

Then the world went dark as the sun went out, and the stars turned their gazes to a new place.

The Thunderbird

I am a fresh-faced, green-blooded bundle of nerves as I fidget on the steps of the headquarters of Myth Control, my clenched hands molding fingerprints into the cardboard cup carrier that holds two steaming coffees. Today is my first official field mission and the day that I meet my new partner Michael. I strain my ears, listening for the sound of his car. He should be arriving any minute now.

We've never spoken before. I've been busy finishing up the field training program, and he just returned from extended leave following his last mission, which was successful but proved fatal for his old partner. I can only imagine how raw that wound must be for him, to have lost the mage he trusted with his life every day. I can't fill a void like that, but I'm hoping the fresh coffee will help me make a good first impression, even if it is the cheap cafeteria stuff. I figure that Michael has had worse, given he's a seasoned hunter who's been into the wilderness and survived on field rations more times than most people have gone into their own backyards. And he'll appreciate the early-morning shot of caffeine.

I should be less excited out of respect for Michael's recent loss, but the very thought of going into the field and finally seeing these magnificent creatures alive and with my own eyes has me fidgeting and bouncing on my feet. And the very first one I'm going to see is a *thunderbird*. A rare, elusive, beautiful thunderbird.

My pulse feels as electric as the lightning that's said to trail from the creature's wings.

I'm so distracted by my own excitement that I miss the signs of Michael's approach, and his car is pulling around the last bend in the driveway before I realize he's there. The engine growls as the Jeep sails up the last leg of the hill, roof lights blazing and putting the still-rising sun to shame. I go still as this mechanical beast rumbles to a halt in front of me, all four massive tires chewing on the gravel. The engine cuts and the far door opens and slams. Footsteps crackle around the front of the car, and a man broad and hard enough to be worthy of this machine comes into view. He is dressed in the heavy green jacket and cargo pants Myth Control issues to its field agents. His head is crowned with thick, black hair, and the planes of his face are straight and sharp. Despite the darkness of the morning, sunglasses obscure his eyes, but I sense the once-over he gives me as he steps forward. He is not impressed. I feel very small before him.

"You my new Kate?" he asks.

My mind is blank for a moment before my memory jolts into action. Kate was the name of his former partner. The one who died. "Yes," I blurt. "New mage. I'm Morgan." I thrust my hand out and step forward. I stumble when my foot drops lower than I'm expecting. I've forgotten that I'm still on the stairs, and I only just manage to stop myself from faceplanting into the gravel driveway.

I fail to stop the coffee.

Both cups go sailing out of the carrier. One of them bounces off of Michael's arm before exploding on the ground, splattering both of our legs in hot liquid. The other hits Michael square in the chest and blasts open. I stare in mortified fascination as the coffee seeps into his clothes and scalds his face. He yelps in pain, and my brain unhelpfully decides that maybe coffee was the wrong choice for a good first impression.

We leave headquarters a little over thirty minutes later. The sun is up in the blue summer sky, fresh mountain air pours through the open frame of the Jeep, and Michael's face and hands shine with the burn ointment from the infirmary. He wasn't badly hurt, but the look he gave me while the nurse slathered the cream on was so scathing, I almost asked for some of the ointment for myself.

"Mages are more trouble than they're worth," he growled before stalking out of the infirmary.

Those are the only words he's said to me thus far, so the ride out from headquarters is an awkward one. I try to get a conversation going at first, but I'm mostly just yelling that I'm really, really sorry over the roar of the wind coming into the Jeep. Michael presses his mouth into a thin line in response, and I take the hint and let the wind shut me up. That gives me plenty of time to wonder if any other mages have ever screwed up their jobs so quickly and efficiently. I don't think they have.

Michael steers the Jeep along the path the GPS carves out for us, following the intel from headquarters. We're a little behind schedule thanks to the impromptu coffee shower, but it isn't long before we sight low storm clouds between the mountains. Michael keeps to the main roads as he takes us down into the valley. The wind picks up and rolls the scent of petrichor through the Jeep, and I taste a crack of lightning on my tongue. Some of my earlier excitement returns, and I yell to Michael that we're close to our target.

"Imagine that," he shouts back, and I could cut myself on the edge of the irritation in his voice.

Right. Of course he's aware of that. He's a seasoned hunter with a capture record longer than I am tall. He knows what he's doing.

The rain starts to fall not long after that. It drums on the roof of the Jeep and slants in through the open door frames, cold in spite of the summer weather. Lightning flashes overhead, chased by a crack of thunder. I lean forward to peer through the top of the windshield, and catch a glimpse of a swirling path of unnatural wind cutting through the dark clouds.

Michael sees it too. He turns the Jeep to follow, taking us off the road. He's forced to slow down as the car picks its way over the rocky terrain, but we're still moving much faster than I would consider safe. I bounce in my seat and grip the edge of the roof, each drop snapping my teeth together and rattling my brain in my skull. I feel nausea rising as the Jeep tears its way over fallen trees and broken boulders, and my spine is shrieking in protest from my neck all the way to my tailbone. Michael keeps his eyes trained on the sky and steers the car through raw instinct and genuine trust in the flexibility of the axles.

Eventually, blessedly, the ground flattens out beneath the wheels, and the Jeep bursts on to the rain-soaked shore of a wide lake. The storm has ripped the surface of the water into a gray frenzy that flashes with a brittle sheen beneath the lightning. At the edge of the water, a boat bangs against a small wooden dock. Lightning flashes again overhead, and the dark shape of the thunderbird resolves herself inside the clouds, wings spread and talons bared. The clap of thunder that follows isn't enough to drown out her hunting cry.

The Jeep skids on the sand as Michael hits the breaks. My seatbelt digs into my neck as I shoot forward, but I can't take my eyes off of the thunderbird as she descends out of the boiling sky.

She is beautiful, with lightning crackling along her sleek, black feathers from her beak all the way to her tail, where it sparks and forks in a dazzling trail behind her. Her wings are sharp and angular, and they cut the wind like a knife. Thunder sounds when she flaps her wings, and I catch the vibrant flash of her eye as she circles over the lake, a tiny blue pinprick against her gloriously dark plumage.

"Stop gawking," Michael snaps, "and get this ready." He throws a net into my lap before leaping out the door.

I blink at the heavy net, then at the open driver's side door, then at Michael's receding form as he races over the sand, heading for the dock. My mouth goes dry.

Surely he's read the file from Myth Control. He has to know the details about my magic and what it can and cannot do. He couldn't have *not* read the file. That would be gross negligence.

But he gave me the net and told me to get it ready, and now he's running headlong at a thunderbird without any magical or physical protection on him.

I throw open the door of the Jeep and jump to the ground, jarring my knees on impact. I get myself up as quickly as I can and stumble after Michael, dragging the net after me. I feel a greasy residue building on my hands, the kind that comes from an old spell that's starting to unravel. I think it's a fireproofing spell on the net, and Michael wants me to reinforce the magic.

I cannot do that. I have to warn him.

The thunderbird shrieks and descends on the little boat just as Michael gets to the dock, and something large and stocky goes flopping over the side of the boat into the water. Michael is there in an instant, snatching up and brandishing one of the oars from the rocking boat. It's the right choice; the plastic head of the oar smokes and melts when it makes brief contact with the thunderbird's chest, but it does not conduct her lightning. With a scream and a thunderclap of her wings, she rises up and banks hard in the air, moving out over the lake.

Michael is already in the boat and revving the tiny motor by the time I reach the dock. The motor gives a blurry roar, and he sets off. I leap after him, pulling the net with me, and just manage to land inside the boat as it pulls away from the dock. It rocks violently with my landing, nearly sending me headlong into the water, but there's a tug on the net that catches me, and I turn to see that Michael has one hand wrapped in the net and a wild smile on his lips as he pushes the little boat to top speed. Over his shoulder, I see a stocky man decked out in fishing gear slosh to his feet near the dock. His mouth hangs open as he stares after us, eyes blank with the special kind of horror that can only touch those who have just had a mythical creature try to snatch them out of their boat and carry them off as breakfast. Then the boat is bouncing over the rough lake and the rain is lashing my skin, and I have to bury my face in my arm to shield it from the stinging rain.

Before long, another cry from the thunderbird rips across the lake, and the boat slows enough for me to raise my head and peer ahead. The thunderbird is circling in a wide arc, watching us with her bright eyes. She screams again, and then she is streaking low over the water, coming right for us, wings spread and lightning sparking off her feathers.

I don't have time to be afraid. Michael yanks on the net, pulling me over backwards and sending me sprawling on the wet floor of the dinghy. He's on his feet and rocking with the boat, riding the rough motion with graceful ease as he gathers the net in his hands, getting ready to throw.

Dimly, I think to myself that I should stop him, because thunderbirds and lakes do not mix and she'll die if she falls into the water and that's not what this mission is for, and then I remember that Michael thinks the fireproofing spell on the net is strong enough to hold.

"Wait!" I cry as Michael brings his arm back.

He does not hear me. He swings forward and lets the net fly. It opens over the thunderbird as she comes in close, and she shows no fear in the face of the sudden obstacle. Her lightning flashes and scorches the net to ash, and then she is before us, talons up and raking the air as she slashes at Michael, and I'm on my feet and slamming

Michael over the edge of the boat.

We hit the water hard, and a cold jet blasts its way down my throat. I fight off the panicked urge to breathe before my head can break the surface. I come up coughing and spitting water, and hear Michael's rough hacking not far from me. In front of us, the little boat is capsized, a large scorch mark dragging across the belly where the thunderbird touched it. I whip around, frantically searching for her, but the thunderbird is uninterested in continuing her encounter with us. She is climbing back into the clouds and does not spare us another look before she disappears. The rain quickly lets up as the clouds roll after her, leaving a crystal blue sky in their wake. The lake quiets in the thunderbird's absence, becoming glassy and calm, disturbed only by our ripples as Michael and I tread water.

I feel a breathless wash of relief as I stare after the rapidly receding storm clouds. The thunderbird was safely chased off, I stopped Michael from getting gored, and now that I can see our surroundings, I'm realizing how beautiful this valley lake is, with the mountains rising all around and the greens and golds of the trees on the shore reflected on the pristine surface of the water.

Then a cold splash smacks across my face, and I cough more lake water out of my nose and mouth.

"The hell was that?" Michael demands. He's lost his sunglasses to the lake, and without their dark shields in place, the full intensity of his scathing stare bores into me.

I freeze under that glare. My face slips into the water, shocking me back to my senses, and I kick hard, propelling myself back up. "The net failed," I said. "The spell wasn't set, and the thunderbird burned clean through it."

Michael's expression darkens as he surveys the capsized boat and the burn on the hull. "I told you to prep the net." His eyes are razor sharp when they fix on me again. "Do you think this is a game?"

I flounder in the water again and sputter, "Of course not! I was trying to help!"

"Helping would have been doing your job and resetting the spell on the net, like I told you."

"I don't do that," I say.

Michael gives me an incredulous stare. "The hell did you just say to me?" He swims closer, and I recoil so fast, my arms slap the water and douse me all over again. "You're a rookie mage," he growls. "You're *only job* is to help your hunter with all the magical crap so he can focus on taking these monsters down. And when you're hunter tells you to do something, *you do it*."

"That's not what I—"

"Kid, how thick is your skull that—"

"I can't do physical magic!" I shout. The words are punctured by a hard splash as I flail in the water, and the world is silent in their wake. "It's not in my skillset."

Michael's gaze goes flat. "They gave me a mage that can't do magic."

"*Physical* magic," I huff, weary from keeping myself afloat. "I can't bind your equipment or cast safety spells, but for me, tracking and mental magics are like breathing." The metaphor would be stronger if I wasn't gasping between words, but it's true. I hold the highest scores in those areas across the entire region, and I tested top three in the country. "This was all in my file," I say to Michael. "Didn't you read it?"

Michael says nothing. Instead, he gives the capsized boat a moment of consideration, then turns and starts swimming for the shore. He pulls away from me quickly, and I know I'll never get that boat righted on my own. I have no choice but to follow him.

I don't think he read my file.

The long swim back gives me plenty of time to bring my own anger to a simmering boil. He *should* have read my file. He *should* have been prepared. He said it himself; he's the hunter and the leader of the team. Why didn't he read it?

The answer comes to me halfway back to shore.

Michael is an experienced hunter with a massive list of captures and kills to his name, all done with his old partner Kate casting at his side. He's accustomed to being able to rely on his mage for everything he's ever needed. I'm the outlier here, the one with the unique brand of limited magic that Michael never needed to compensate for before. Kate, like most mages sent into the field, was a master of many magics. I am not. And when it came down to it, Kate's kind of magic would have carried the day here. My kind of magic means nothing when a thunderbird is shooting lightning at my partner's face and trying to rip his guts out.

Maybe I was a little too quick to be excited for this job.

By the time I slog myself up onto the shore, the indignant anger I felt is nothing but a cold memory in the pit of my stomach. I allow myself a few moments to catch my breath, then force myself forward with the intent of apologizing to Michael. I owe him that much, but he's busy being accosted by one very frantic, very confused fisherman.

"What the hell was that thing?" the fisherman is yelling. His arms are waving at nothing in particular and he is dangerously close to Michael. "Was it trying to *eat* me? Was it a vulture? Don't they only eat dead things? What did you do with my boat?"

As I hurry over, the fisherman ricochets between asking questions about the thunderbird and demanding to know how he is going to be reimbursed for the damage done to his little dinghy. I suppose that boat is the only rational thing he has to hold on to right now, but from Michael's exasperated sneer, that does not seem to matter in the grand scheme of things. And with the thunderbird on the move, we don't have time for this. I know what I need to do.

I raise my hands as I step up to the two men, my fingers already crooked into position. "I'll handle this," I say to Michael, trying to get between him and the fisherman who is now threatening legal action for absconding with his boat and leaving it capsized in the middle of the lake.

"By all means," Michael growls as he takes a large step back, "let's see what else you can screw up today."

My face burns and my gaze hitches on the large coffee stain on Michael's shirt. The lake swim did not wash it out.

With tension tight across my shoulders, I snag my fingers in the mental energies around the fisherman's head. He flinches and looks ready to punch me as my hands invade his personal space, but as I start tugging on the threads of his memory, his eyes turn glassy and distant and his mouth goes slack. I relax a little as I begin weaving a new pattern across his thoughts, hooking my fingers around the lines and pulling them across each other. I unravel the past half-hour of the man's memory, letting myself fall into the rhythm of the magic working. I shed the last of my embarrassment. I may not be able to reinforce protection spells or successfully navigate staircases while holding hot coffee, but this I understand. I'm careful to only rethread the most recent memories on the surface of the fisherman's mind, leaving the rest of his life untouched and intact. My fingers are light and delicate with the threads, and after a few moments, I tie the final knot. When I snap my fingers to complete the spell, the fisherman shakes back into focus.

He stumbles back and takes a long, bewildered look around before asking if I saw that huge vulture attack him out on the lake. "Damn near ripped my head off," he says. "Made me flip the boat and then wouldn't let me get close enough to turn it back over. Had to swim all the way back to shore!"

"That's right, buddy," I say, adding a soothing pitch to my voice, "and we're from Animal Control. We've been chasing that rabid vulture all over the place, but we'll get her, I promise."

I have no idea if vultures can actually get rabies or not, but this fisherman seems willing to believe it. He thanks me enthusiastically before wandering off in the direction of a Range Rover parked some distance away. I turn to watch him go, and find Michael staring at me with the same intensity but none of the cutting anger as before.

"Mental magics and tracking, huh?" he asks.

I nod vigorously.

Michael scratches his chin and studies me with undisguised intrigue. "I may have use for you, after all."

It takes me a moment to interpret that as a joke, but by the time I start to smile, Michael is already hiking back to where he parked the Jeep. I jog to catch up.

"Can you track this thunderbird?" Michael asks as we reach the car. At my confident nod, he gives the sky a quick survey. "How long will that take?"

I glance up at the clear sky, fully innocent of any traces of a storm. "I'll need a few minutes," I admit.

Michael makes a displeased noise, but he leans against the Jeep and gestures for me to go on.

I waste no time. I let my eyes slip half-closed, turning the world muted and fuzzy, but the traces of magic begin to glow at the corners of my vision. I turn in their direction, taking deep breaths and searching for the taste of rain and lightning on the wind. I catch the fading scent of the thunderbird's storm clouds and study the shape of the breezes over the lake, letting myself get lost in my observations and speculations. The air that tastes like myths is cold and sharp against the summer day, tinged with pine needles. The wind currents swirl over the lake, disrupted by the abrupt change from land to water, but there's a thread of lightning cutting a jagged path towards one of the lower mountains. I close my eyes completely and smell the distance that wind has traveled to carry the trail of the fleeing thunderbird to me. She's moving fast, but there's a definitive pattern to her flight. She knows where she's going. I'll need to check a topographical map of the area and confirm her storm trail against local weather reports, but I'd bet a dangerously large amount of money that she's got a nest a little north and east of where we are now.

I open my eyes and relay my findings to Michael.

He does not look entirely convinced, but he shrugs and climbs up behind the Jeep's steering wheel. "Let's see if you've earned your keep," he says, slamming the door behind him.

I manage to clamber into my seat and get the door closed just as Michael hits the gas and takes us away from the lake. To my relief, he sticks to an actual road this time, although it's little more than an uneven ribbon of dirt between the trees. It's far smoother than the off-road descent we took earlier, though, and it isn't long before we bump back on to tarmac and Michael turns us north.

"I'm sorry about the net and tackling you into the lake," I say, remembering my earlier intention to apologize. "And the coffee. I'm not usually so…"

"Disaster-prone?" Michael quirks an eyebrow. "Kid, you find me that monster and all is forgiven." A moment passes before he adds, "At least for today," but I'm already reaching for the topography maps and the radio and don't think much of it.

I eagerly scan the maps as the local weather station drones in the background. I have to strain a bit to hear it over the wind, but I catch enough to confirm that freak, flash thunderstorms are rolling through the areas between us and where I think the thunderbird is nesting. It's a fast-moving storm system, and the weather reporter seems mildly puzzled that it's not following typical weather patterns, but not enough to really be interested. I smirk when I point this out to Michael.

"It's good most people are willfully blind to all this magical stuff," Michael says. "Otherwise, I'd have you working your memory spell all day."

The smile melts off of my face as I slowly realize that he is serious. "I mean, if they actually *saw* the creatures like that guy back at the lake, then absolutely, but that's not really what Myth Control wants me doing."

Michael's eyes narrow and harden, but he keeps his attention on the road. "You're not running training simulations at headquarters anymore, kid. You're out in the field with the monsters, and you need to do whatever it takes."

"I know," I say, "but memory work like that is delicate stuff. One wrong move, and I could have left that guy drooling in the dirt."

"Might have been an improvement," Michael grunts. "So, are you telling me that was a one-time thing, and you're never using memory magic again?"

"Well, if I *need* to, I will. And I am good at it, so I know I wouldn't really have wiped that guy clean, not when I was standing that close to him, but—"

"Answer the question," Michael says. "If I tell you to do memory magic again, will you do it?"

I hesitate, giving Michael a sidelong glance. "If I really need to—"

"Say I'm telling you that you need to do it, or our mission fails."

I blink. "Well, yes, of course I would do it then."

"Good." Michael visibly relaxes, the color returning to his knuckles as his grip loosens on the steering wheel. "I've been out here a long time, kid, seen a lot of monsters and all the nightmares they bring with 'em, and when I tell you that you need to do something, you do it or you die. Understand?"

I nod, but I spend a long while thinking about that.

I know he's right, in the end. I'm part of Myth Control, the government's best-kept secret, and when they send hunter-mage teams like Michael and me out, they expect us to keep mythical creatures separate from the mortal population. If we do our jobs right, most nonmagical folks live their entire lives without knowing that unicorns are real, and during mating season, they can do a lot more damage to your neighborhood than a pair of fighting dragons. At least the dragons stick to high altitudes.

So do thunderbirds, usually, except on the days when they're dropping out of the sky, trying to snatch up unwary fishermen to take back to their nests to feed their hungry, growing chicks.

I love mythical creatures great and small, but now that I'm out in the field and in reality, I have to recognize that they're wild and dangerous. This thunderbird is no exception. That's why Myth Control sent Michael and me after her in the first place. They want us to capture the thunderbird and her chick, and relocate them further into the mountains. Michael has the field record and experience, I am an excellent tracker, and that thunderbird is a beautiful, terrible creature who could slice me apart with her talons or burn me to ashes with lightning, and she's been having a lot of trouble since her chick hatched.

Her territory has always consisted of this cold stretch of mountains. When she was alone, that was enough for her. She hunted on the mountains, and she was about as harmless as her species can be. Her storm patterns actually benefitted the local farmers in the valleys, bringing them a steady and reliable source of rain throughout the year. Now that she has the chick to feed, the thunderbird has shifted her hunting grounds, and gotten a lot less picky about the prey she brings back to her nest. She's been skirting closer and closer to the lowlands, making off with cows, sheep, and one very unlucky dog that decided to bark at the bad weather instead of running from it. But no humans yet. That means there's still time, and we don't need to eliminate her. All Michael and I need to do is catch her, tranquilize her, and relocate her and her nest to the northeastern edge of her territory where the deer and moose populations are healthy enough to sustain both her and her chick for years to come, all without getting ourselves killed in the process.

Michael has a lot more experience than I do, and he's right; I either do what he says, or I die. I need to remember that.

It takes us about an hour to firmly set ourselves back on the thunderbird's trail. The terrain is too extreme even for the Jeep, so we have to stick to the main roads. Michael is not thrilled by the delay, and his fingers drum on the steering wheel as the minutes and the miles slip by. But I can taste raw lightning on the wind now, and I know we're close. I twist in my seat to take inventory of the hunting supplies in the back of the Jeep.

"We've got two nets left," I say, catching Michael's attention. He does not take his eyes off the road, but his head tilts in my direction. I reach out and touch the nets, noting the strong presence of magic over the closer one. "This one has a lower level fireproofing spell than the first net did, but it's fully set. If we can launch it before the thunderbird can generate lightning in her wings, it should hold."

Michael shakes his head. "That monster's going to be a lot more aggressive at the nest than it was out on the lake. We're not going to get the chance to net it before it zaps us. We go on the offense this time."

"But the chick is there," I point out. "We can't risk hurting the baby."

Michael snorts. "Baby's first thunderbolt could stop a bear's heart."

I drop back into my seat, frustrated once more by my lack of physical magic. Another mage would have been able to strengthen the nets, but with me as the magic-user, it looks like we'll need to rely on tranquilizers and hope they're strong enough to last us through the relocation. That still leaves us with the problem of not having a plan of approach. "What should we do?" I ask.

Michael taps the steering wheel again, but the gesture is thoughtful this time rather than impatient. "Can you work your memory magic on monsters or just people?"

I frown, thinking hard. "I've never tried on a mythical creature before, but… I think I could, if I had enough time to set the spell up properly." I glance up at the sky, still void of clouds. "I don't know if changing the thunderbird's memories is going to do what we need, though. I suppose I can make her forget that she's seen us before, but we'd still be invading her territory and coming close to her nest. That's not going to stop her from getting aggressive." I drum my fingers against my knee. "Unless I change what she's seeing," I muse.

Michael frowns. "Thought vanishing spells were physical magic," he says.

"Not if I'm just making the target *think* there's nothing there."

He mulls this over for a long moment. "So, when we're approaching the thunderbird, you edit us out of her vision? Make her think we're a couple of deer?"

"Or just not there at all," I suggest. "Whatever is less likely to make her want to eat us."

Michael gives me an impressed glance. "Could you really do that?"

I nod, slowly at first, then faster. It would take a lot of finesse, but I could use a memory spell as the base, and make the thunderbird believe that she's seeing an empty forest around her. She knows what her territory looks like. I just need to use her own memory as a visual block against something new creeping into her territory. Something like us. As long as we're quiet, this should work.

"I'll need to be pretty close to throw the spell correctly," I say, shaping my fingers around the new magic. "Maybe a couple hundred feet at most. It would be cleaner and faster if I'm closer than that, but I think that's the edge of our safety line. If you can give me the time, I can work the spell from a distance."

"As long as this monster can't see us coming, you take all the time you need."

We spend the next several miles talking over our plan of approach, including how far I can stretch my magic and what else we should expect to find living in a thunderbird's territory. I'm feeling more and more confident in myself as we work out each detail, and Michael is looking more and more optimistic as we drive on.

"You know, kid, I'm glad you understand what's really going on here," Michael says at one point. "I don't think a lot of mages *or* hunters fully get it. Hell, *I* didn't get it at first, but once you take down your first monster, it all clicks into place."

His expression goes distant for a moment, as though remembering other hunts he's been on, ones with a different mage in the passenger seat.

I know that I have a long way to go before I can actually fill Kate's place as a good partner to Michael, but I'm determined to make my first hunt a success. I keep working on the base shape of the new spell, making adjustments whenever I find a piece that doesn't quite fit right. The hardest part is trying not to mind the silence that's settled over us.

We pass a few more miles in that silence, following the road as it leads us further into the mountains, but it's not long before we crest an incline and see the dark gathering of clouds ahead. Michael whoops and taps the horn a few times, breaking my concentration for a moment, but his excitement is infectious and I'm smiling as I get back to work.

Michael steers the Jeep down the slope, taking us to a lonely stretch of highway that runs along the side of a mountain. The clouds are boiling in the sky in front of us, a dark curtain of rain falling from their bellies. He parks on the side of the road and leaves the Jeep idling while he jumps out and runs around to the back.

"Need help?" I call after him, a bit half-heartedly. The spell is finally starting to come together around my fingers, and I'm reluctant to drop it.

"Nah," Michael says. "You relax and get your magic ready. I'm gonna need it!"

I'm glad that Michael can't see me blush. My stomach is fluttering with nerves, so I take a few deep breaths to calm myself. I'm good at this kind of magic. I can do this.

I'm finishing the last flourishes of the memory spell when Michael slips back into the front seat, an unloaded rifle slung across his lap. He opens a box of ammunition, and I watch him idly, letting the rhythm of his hands feed into the final patterns of the spell. I've got the shape down, and I can finally see how to tie it off when I use it on the thunderbird. I release the magic but hold the pattern in my mind as I refocus on the world around me, starting with Michael's hands as he loads the rifle. I freeze when I realize he's not putting tranquilizers into the gun.

"Michael?" I say, my voice scratching in my throat. "What are you doing?"

"Getting ready for the hunt," he says, as though this is the most natural thing in the world. I suppose, to him, it is, but…

"This is a live capture," I say. "Why are you loading bullets?"

Michael stops and looks at me with genuine surprise. He quirks a confused half-smile, as though he thinks I'm joking. It falters when he realizes that I am not. Then he sighs, disappointed. "I see. You *don't* understand."

"The mission briefing?" I ask. "No, I read the dossier, and it said to relocate the thunderbird nest. We're not authorized to use deadly force."

Michael deliberately finishes loading the gun and rests it across his lap before he turns to me. "I thought we were clear on this: you do what I say, or you die."

"But if I work this memory spell like we were planning, we won't be in serious danger, and you'll have the time you need to tranq the mother *and* the chick."

Michael tilts his head. "Kid, you're still doing that magic. Nothing's changed here."

"But why the bullets? We're not here to kill her!"

Michael swivels so that he is fully facing me in his seat. "Yes," he says quietly, "we are."

I shake my head, slowly at first, then faster. "Michael, you know that these creatures are vital parts of the ecosystem. We're only supposed to put them down if the populations are getting out of control, or if they're directly threatening human lives."

Michael tilts his head and studies me for a moment. "I can see you're going to need a little more convincing, and the whole 'monsters are *always* a threat to human lives' spiel isn't going to cut it." A wicked smirk cuts across his face. "I used that on Kate, and it took her so long to actually understand me." He shrugs. "But it was too late for her by then."

I go very still under Michael's gaze. "What are you talking about?"

"Come on, kid, you erase memories and write new ones. You gotta be smart for that. Definitely smarter than Kate was, so I'm counting on you to understand me here."

He gives me a few moments to think.

Did Kate make a wrong move out in the field? Is that why a chimera got her on their last hunt? The details around her death had been hazy, but it was definitely chimera venom that killed her. She must have been careless to get herself bitten while not carrying any antivenom in her gear. Strange, though, that an experienced mage would make that kind of mistake.

"Look," I say, "I know you're hurting after what happened to Kate. I know you're angry and if I was in your place, maybe I'd want to hunt down every predatory creature in the state, too. But this isn't a monster we're tracking. She's not even a chimera! All we need…"

I trail off as Michael chuckles.

"Kid, there was no chimera. Not a live one, anyway."

For a moment, I forget how to speak. My brain feels foggy when I finally manage to form words again. "But they found venom in Kate's system."

Michael smirks. "Imagine that."

My gaze flashes between Michael's eyes and the gun in his lap. "You mean, you…?"

"I knew you were smart." Michael settles back into his seat and looks calmly at the sky. "Kate had been on my case for months, complaining about how our hunts always seemed to end with kill shots instead of captures. She thought the same thing you do, that these monsters somehow deserve to live, but they're nothing but nightmares, and you never get a better rush than watching the life drain out of a nightmare." He smiles and closes his eyes. "I like it when they die slow. You can see the magic leaking out of them, all pretty and lit up like fireflies. Kate didn't like that.

"I'm not an unreasonable man. I told her she didn't have to die, but she stopped doing what I told her to, and that meant she wasn't useful anymore." He opens his eyes and turns his head to look at me again, letting it roll lazily over the seat's headrest. "You could still be useful to me, way more than Kate ever was. *Kate* couldn't erase memories, so I couldn't count on her to help me deal with those soft-gutted suits back at headquarters who kept scolding me for killing all the monsters. Hated it whenever I had to bring in a live capture to shut them up. But now I've got you, and you're too smart to make the same mistake Kate did." He smiles, showing far too many teeth. "Or do I need to get rid of you, too?"

My gut twists, but my body is numb and sluggish and will not respond to my frantic internal screams.

"Can't say it was a chimera again, they don't live this far north." Michael scratches his chin as he studies me. "Suppose the bird could get you, and a drop from the sky would explain a broken neck. Or those talons could open your guts."

The teasing lilt to his voice makes me think that he's trying to intimidate me into submission, but instinct warns me that he's actually planning aloud how he's going to kill me if I disobey. If I don't help him slaughter these creatures. That's enough to get my body moving again. I lunge across the seats, going for the gun.

Michael is faster. He whips the rifle out of my reach while his other hand closes around my wrist and yanks me off balance. Then he lunges forward, slamming me back against the passenger door in the same fluid motion he uses to gently deposit the rifle on to the back seat. Pain flares across my shoulder and panicked sweat breaks out on my brow. Michael leans closer and gives me a stern look. "Bullet holes would be a lot harder to explain," he growls, "but I can come up with something if I have to." He jams me harder against the door, and I whimper. "Are you going to make me do that, or are you going to be a good little mage, and do what I tell you?"

My hand scrapes across the door handle, and then the door swings wide as I tumble out of the Jeep. It's a long fall, and the momentum rips me out of Michael's grip. I hear him curse just before I land on the tarmac, a dull jolt vibrating through my arm. I try to crawl away before Michael can come after me, but my shoulder screams in protest. Something is fractured, if not broken, and I'm not going to get very far before the hunter with the loaded gun comes after me. I have to find another way. I push myself to sit up. Pain flares again across my injury, and the pattern of the memory spell I've been holding at the back of my mind suddenly burns across my vision.

I know what I need to do.

I raise my uninjured arm just as Michael's face appears above me, and I rip at the mental strands rippling out from him, tugging them hard into a new alignment. Michael flinches, and his eyes go wide as he realizes what I'm doing. The anger burns freely in him, and he has enough time to bring the gun to bear on me, but that's all. His gaze goes distant and glassy as I twist his memories and pull myself from his sight. I am not gentle. I do not have time to be. The spell is ragged and fragile and so close to coming undone, but I think of the thunderbird, and of Kate, and of myself, and I find the strength I need to pull the threads into place and tie the final knot. I snap my fingers, and I am done.

I keep very still as Michael shudders and shakes himself. His eyes slip back into focus and lock on me, and he frowns. I hold my breath, not allowing myself even that small movement. Michael shakes his head again, blinks a few times, and then he looks past me. He spends a few moments orienting himself, and I can see his confusion warring against the new memory I've woven of him not even going to headquarters this morning, and deciding to go after the thunderbird alone. He's a seasoned hunter, after all. What does he need a mage for? They're far more trouble than they're worth.

My heart is bruising itself against my ribs as I wait for Michael to either accept the change, or fight it off and remember that I am here, and he wants to kill me.

Then, still frowning, Michael pulls the door of the Jeep closed, and I lose sight of him. There's a dangerous pause, and then I hear the gear shift and the parking break release. I move my legs out of the way as the Jeep rolls away, gathering speed as Michael hits the gas. I take a ragged, choking breath as the car speeds down the road.

The Jeep has disappeared by the time I manage to pick myself up. I gently brush myself off, wincing as I discover the bloody scrapes where my skin met the asphalt. I look at the storm ahead of me, the one Michael is rushing to meet, and I can't help but feel a little sick at what I've done.

I wasn't very precise when I worked that spell, and I wasn't just thinking of me when I modified Michael's mind. I didn't go deep enough to rip out Kate, but the thunderbird…

Michael still knows where her nest is. He still knows that he's hunting her. But he no longer remembers how to recognize her, or the shape she cuts across the sky and the thundercrack of her scream as she dives, talons out and ready. There's a good chance he won't see her coming until it's too late.

I watch the rain for a few minutes, long enough to see a lightning bolt rip across the clouds. I can't see the thunderbird or the Jeep or where this storm ends, but I can see that Michael was right about one thing: we're supposed to kill monsters.

And I've done my job today.

The Beetle
and the Twins

In a forest soaked with magic and overrun with unicorns, basilisks, chimeras, and too many other species to name, there lived a perfectly ordinary, nonmagical beetle.

It lived as uneventful a life as a beetle in a magical forest could live. There were days when the beetle found itself inconvenienced by things the magic touched, but ultimately, there was little difference between a bluebird and a phoenix when both shared the end goal of eating a beetle, just as there was little difference between catching a ride on a plain red fox and catching a ride on a three-tailed kitsune in fox form. The beetle managed these things the same way its magic-touched fellows did: by scurrying fast and hiding well and clinging with all its strength. The only difference was that our beetle did not speak while it went about its day, or leave a trail of gemstone dust in its wake. Our beetle was smart enough not to envy its magic-touched fellows, for a yelling beetle leaving a trail of glitter through the forest is very easy for bluebirds *and* phoenixes to follow.

So, the beetle went about its days, doing all of the things that nonmagical beetles get up to, along with some of the things the magical ones do. Our beetle was fairly content with its life in the forest, about as content as you'd imagine a beetle could be.

Until, that is, the twins came.

Their arrival was particularly ill-timed for our beetle, who had been experiencing as near-perfect a day as possible for a bug in a magic-riddled forest. The beetle was enjoying a small patch of late afternoon sunshine. Once its body was sufficiently warmed, it planned to head back into the shade and go visit a peer who had seemed very interested in creating more beetles the last time they'd met. Our beetle was rather looking forward to their next rendezvous when four large boots came stomping out of the undergrowth.

One boot came dangerously close to crushing the little bug, and our beetle wisely doubted that its shell would protect it from adventurers in a careless hurry. So the beetle scurried back, intending to take shelter under a nearby thorn bush. But the boot ripped up out of the ground and flipped the beetle on to its back. Its legs beat angrily at the branches and leaves laced across the pale sky. It was always such a bother, getting stuck upside-down, but our beetle had experience with this sort of predicament. It wriggled on the soft ground, trying to find enough purchase to roll itself back over. Based on the grinding sensation against its shell, the beetle surmised that it had either been knocked against a rock—unlikely, considering the give of the earth around it—or into one of the glitter trails left by one of those sparkly, magic-stained insects. It would have preferred the rock.

By the time the beetle managed to right itself, two identical elven faces were pressed close overhead, staring at the beetle and muttering to each other.

The beetle tried to pay them no mind. It had come across elves, humans, and dwarves in the forest before. Mostly dead ones, thanks to the thriving chimera population, but live ones would occasionally appear between the trees. These adventurers often hunted the gemstone beetles and left our little one well enough alone, so it was quite odd that these two had decided that this particular bug was worth their intense scrutiny.

"It has to be this one," one of the elves said. A broad grin split his white face, and his dark eyes danced merrily.

"I'm not so sure," his twin said, frowning deeply under severe eyebrows. His fine, golden hair was pulled back behind his pointed ears and bound with a thin strip of leather, exactly the same as his twin's. They even dressed identically, the beetle observed, in deep green tunics with brown belts and trousers, and sturdy, heavy, dangerous-for-a-beetle boots.

"Look at the markings," the smiling elf insisted. "We've searched this entire forest and never seen another beetle like this one."

"But are they the *right* markings?" the frowning elf asked.

The beetle was confused by all of this, for it had no special markings upon its shell. Its shell was a particularly deep black, of which the beetle was very proud and went to great lengths to maintain, but it was a uniform black. At least, it would be, once the beetle had cleaned off the streak of ruby glitter currently residing back there.

The beetle shivered, hating the feeling of the residue on its shell. Now it would need to go to the pond before visiting its amorous friend. Our beetle took a moment to orient itself against a growth of glowing moss on a nearby tree, then turned and started in the direction of the pond.

The smiling elf dropped his smile and leapt in front of the beetle, drawing an arrow from the quiver on his back and nocking his bow in one smooth motion. "Hold it right there, little one, or this arrow will split you in half." He was frowning intently now.

"And if his fails," the other elf said, now grinning manically behind his own loaded bow, "mine will not."

Shooting arrows struck the beetle as a particularly foolish way to try to kill a small bug, considering the elves' heavy boots had almost done the job mere minutes earlier, and quite by accident. The beetle doubted that the elves would have much luck with those narrow arrowheads. Still, it did not like the idea of perishing with an unclean shell. And so it halted. It supposed that it could tolerate this nonsense for a little while. The elves had to eventually realize their mistake and go on their way, and then the beetle could continue on with its life. What was a little time wasted when it meant not being squished by an elf's boot?

"Right, then," the twin in front of the beetle said. "Since we caught you, you have to reveal one truth."

"A truth of our asking," the twin behind quickly put in. "Not some random fact you pull out of the air and use to get out of answering our question."

"And answer us straight, not in riddles."

"Or in the form of another question."

The beetle surmised that, since they were adding specific conditions to their demands, the twins had caught a number of talking creatures throughout their adventure in the forest. Nonlinear answers were a favorite tactic among the talking foxes, while the speaking deer preferred to stare at their surroundings and jabber on about their observations. The twins had probably caught a butterfly, too, if they'd had their question answered in the form of another question. That had more to do with the inherent inquisitiveness of butterflies than anything else; they simply had a lot of questions and not a lot of room in their tiny heads to keep the answers.

Our beetle, on the other hand, would be employing none of these tactics. You'll recall that, even rolled in gemstone dust, our beetle was nonmagical, and therefore could not speak.

"We will take your silence as acquiescence to our requests."

The beetle let this pass without so much as a twitch of its leg.

"Now," the elf continued, "why is it that—"

"Hold on," his twin cut in. "Are we *certain* that this is the right beetle?"

The elves' arrows did not twitch away from the beetle as one squinted at it, and the other stared with wide eyes.

"Just as much as you are doubting it," one of the elves finally said, "I am certain that this is the right creature."

"It would be nice if, just once, we both could be a little confident," the other replied.

"You would prefer fractional confidence to utmost certainty?"

"You're the one with the certainty," the frowning elf said. "All I have are doubts."

The other elf sighed. "All right, if I admit that there is a chance that this beetle is *not* the creature the old hermit told us to find…?"

The second one brightened fractionally. "Well, there is always the chance that it *is* the right beetle after all, and there's no harm in asking, right?"

"The curse certainly does not forbid us from that."

The beetle began to wonder how far into the underbrush it could get before the twins realized it was making an escape. Not very far, it concluded, but now that there was a known curse in the equation, the beetle was beginning to think that the risk would be worth it.

"All right, mystical beetle," one of the elves said, "as per the Laws of the Forest set forth by the gods who created this land, may they reign supreme until time has folded back on itself…"

The beetled wondered if this was going to be one of those very long preambles.

It was. The sun slid across the sky, and the beetle felt a few patches of warmth slide over its shell as the sky shifted. Three times, the beetle stood in full sunlight and then deep shade before the elf's speech drew to a close.

"…under the fifth moon of the five hundredth year of the Blue Wolf, I, Ateros of House Silverwood, fifth of my name, and my brother, Soreta of House Silverwood, first of his name, do hereby demand that you tell us how to lift the curse of opposition placed upon our brows at birth by the Fairy Queen our father rejected before marrying our fair mother."

The beetle was impressed at this demonstration of lung capacity. That was the only thing of value that came out of the speech, which had burned much of the afternoon away. The sun was slanting low through the trees now, casting the forest in that special glow that bathed even the nonmagical things in gold. The evening would come before long, and with it a chill that the beetle would prefer to avoid. It was not late enough in the year for the cold to be dangerous, but all the same, a warm, dark burrow was better than a moonlit shiver, and the pond would be unpleasant now. The beetle thought about its amorous friend and wondered if they would mind the glitter still stuck to the back of its shell.

"Oi, beetle," one of the elves said. "We asked you a question."

"Give it a minute," the twin said. "It's thinking."

"How long does a beetle need to think?"

"A good long while, I would expect, if it's going to tell us the proper way to undo this curse."

The beetle thought that even if it possessed the capacity to speak, it would do no such thing. Curses were messy, unpleasant things, and our beetle was too wise to get tangled up in one. Better to wait for the elves to grow bored with this nonsense, or realize their mistake and go bother some other unsuspecting resident of the forest.

The elves did no such thing.

They waited, one fidgeting and the other stock still. They watched the beetle, one directly and the other sidelong. They cycled through moments of conviction and doubt, but did not take their eyes—or their arrows—off of the beetle.

The sun slipped even further down in the sky, and the light began to give way to darkness.

The beetle tapped one leg against the ground, now thinking only of a warm burrow.

"It's been a good long while," one of the elves finally said. "I don't think it's going to answer."

"It still could," his brother said.

"But what if it doesn't know? What if we gave that old hermit the dragon egg for nothing?"

"Well, not *nothing*," the other elf said. "We did get a full week of us both being awake at the same time."

"But it's almost over, and the Dark One's uprising is coming."

The elves were silent for a moment.

"Look," one finally said, "the prophecy clearly states that twin warriors would break the curse of their birth, and rise up to kill the Dark One and his dragon. We are the only cursed-at-birth twins in the entire kingdom."

"And we're almost out of time."

"Yes," the first elf hissed, "hence the wild search for a way to break the curse. Or did you forget the past three years of our lives?"

"Believe me, I haven't, but say we *don't* break the curse? Say we don't waste any more time, and we go after the Dark One anyway?"

"The prophecy is very specific in its—"

"*Hang* the prophecy, and then set it on fire! I say we go find the Dark One while the physical side of this curse is still at bay."

"But we only have until sundown tomorrow until one of us falls asleep again."

"He can't be that hard to find. It's one sinister old man and a dragon."

"But we haven't seen any dragons, or met any sinister old men."

"What about the hermit?"

"He wasn't sinister. Just very, very excited to get that dragon egg."

There was a pause.

"Although, his laugh was a bit throaty, now that I think about it."

"And he lives in the Miasma Bog."

"But we traded him an egg, not a dragon. Certainly, it will hatch someday, but we have plenty of time before that happens."

"Well… say it moved."

"Say what moved?"

"The egg. Right before I handed it to the old man. I felt it… twitch."

"Twitch?"

"Yes."

"Are you saying we gave a twitching dragon egg to an old hermit in the Miasma Bog who understands curses well enough to give us a week's worth of minor freedom from our personal, as-of-yet unbreakable curse in exchange for said egg, and then said hermit sent us on a quest that's thus far proven fruitless?"

"Yes."

"And said sinister old hermit in said Miasma Bog has had nearly a week alone with said twitching dragon egg?"

"Yes."

"And you *knew* it was a twitching dragon egg?"

"Yes."

"Do you not see why you maybe should have said something earlier?"

"Well, I knew it was maybe a bad idea, but I assumed you knew about the egg, too. You sounded so confident in all of your notes."

"What about giving a hatching dragon egg to an evil hermit living in the middle of poisonous purple fog strikes you as the kind of plan that should be carried through with conviction?"

"Oh, so he's *definitely* evil now? He wasn't when you tied me to a horse and set us off on this doomed quest. No, back then, he was only 'eccentric' and 'a little anti-social'."

"Well, you're the one who did all the early research! I didn't say we *had* to go to the Miasma Bog!"

"But you *are* the one who told me to look for an old hermit with knowledge of curses in the first place!"

The elves' voices eventually faded behind the beetle as it scurried further and further away. Its legs felt stiff in the chill of the night, and it would definitely need to wait until tomorrow to clean its shell, let alone drop in on its amorous friend and hope that they had not already found a new partner, but for the moment, the beetle was just glad to be away.

It had certainly had enough of magic for one day.

The Marvel Artist

It was a sleepy afternoon under a patchwork sky when Raine mastered his first marvel. He was quite proud of himself, having lacked a proper teacher throughout his life. There was one other master in Raine's home village, but Raine did not count him as a *proper* teacher as he was old and traditional and boring where Raine was young and fresh and innovative. So Raine had taught himself, pushing and pulling on the fabric of reality and learning to shape it into more pleasing forms, until the day came when he could lift a paintbrush to the sky and leave his mark.

He did not paint anything of particular interest at first. Instead, he blended clouds in and out of existence, smeared sunsets into dramatic flourishes, bled the blue out of the sky in the winter and painted the color back in over the summer. He enjoyed letting his brush idly slip and slide over his canvas, but planned masterpieces in his head. In his mind's eye, he painted sunrises burning with hope and twilights soft with serenity, blazing middays and stoic midnights. He painted skyscapes so many times in his imagination that he grew bored of them, and decided to try something else for his first true marvel work.

Instead of clouds and suns, Raine painted himself over his village. His face bloomed wise and benevolent and dignified across the sky. It was his first portrait, and he was pleased to see how smoothly his skills had manifested, how easily he had been able to translate his brush strokes into portraiture.

The villagers saw his work and, familiar with the workings of marvel artists over many generations, believed that it was a capable portrait, but lacked refinement and real skill. Many of the villagers agreed that young Raine had successfully taught himself to copy the works of other marvel artists, but he had not yet found the heart of his own work. Still, he showed promise, and they were pleased to see a fresh marvel in the village after the old master's retirement some months ago.

They were less pleased when Raine left his portrait in the sky, smiling indulgently down on them from sunup to sundown. The artist made adjustments here and there, but only small, idle ones to a curling lock of hair or the texture of the tunic. The flat face and the self-indulgent smile remained, drawing grumbles from the villagers that grew louder the longer the portrait remained. The farmers especially had thin patience for the portrait, as tilling fields and working plows was considerably less enjoyable with a young man's smug face hovering overhead, never making a sound but somehow constantly suggesting that their techniques were sloppy.

Eventually, some of the bolder members of the village approached Raine with the intent of asking him to paint something new. He had, after all, been working on his self-portrait for well over three weeks now. Surely it was finished, or he was ready to try something new?

It was not, and Raine was not. In fact, some days he simply lay on the grassy hill outside of his home at the edge of the village, staring up at his work and admiring it. He would then add a brush stroke or two, then go back to gazing at his larger-than-life self and feeling a deep sense of satisfaction at the way he had contoured the line of his jaw and placed his eyes directly over the village square, so that his people would always feel his gentle gaze upon them.

He was bewildered, then, when the villagers came and asked him to paint something new.

Maybe he would consider an animal or a flower for his next work. Or perhaps the village leader would commission a portrait of his wife, who was kind and charitable and loved by many. The village would not mind having her in their sky for a month or two, her smile painted across the clouds and the light of the sun behind her eyes.

Raine did not understand. The villagers would rather have a plain-faced woman in the sky instead of his own handsome features?

They would. She was well-known and meant something to them. No, she was not beautiful, but she worked hard and often lent a hand around the village when it was needed, and she took their concerns to the leader, who listened and made improvements based on her advice. Raine's work was certainly impressive, but why leave one portrait of a severe, unfamiliar wizard over the village when there was so much else he could do?

Raine grew quiet then, and thoughtful. He sent the villagers away, but not before promising that he would paint something new by morning.

The villagers went to bed pleased that night, and woke horrified the next day.

True to his word, Raine had changed the portrait in the sky, but instead of the familiar, kindly face of the mayor's wife, Raine had painted a wart-crusted pig in a lumpy dress. Beady eyes stared down at the center square, the jaws lolled to let the red tongue lick at the fields, and the snout leaked thick rain directly on to the leader's house.

The villagers raced to Raine's home to demand that he change the portrait. Even without the inherent ugliness of the boar, the permanent raincloud that had been fixed over the leader's home was bound to cause flooding throughout the village. That, at the very least, needed to be removed. But when they reached the little house on the hill, Raine was gone. He had packed his things and set off for the next town. All he left behind was a broken paintbrush, a note that advised the villagers to develop a better appreciation of real art, and the portrait of the hog in the sky.

Raine traveled for five days and nights before he came upon the next village. This one was on the coast, and with the storms that often rolled in from the sea, they had no use for sky portraits. That was fine, as Raine's painting days were behind him now. It was a silly marvel, anyway, and there were plenty others he could master.

So Raine settled into the new village. He claimed an abandoned hut on the outskirts of the settlement and threw himself into studying and perfecting his next marvel, all the while ignoring the people as best he could. Sometimes, he had to speak with them when he went to get food and new clothing for himself, but he kept these interactions brief and formal. He knew that he had made a mistake in his home village, becoming too familiar with the locals and letting them believe they could make demands of him. Better to be mysterious and aloof and work his marvels from afar. He was, however, pleased to learn that the leader of the coastal village had no wife. With that happy knowledge, Raine shut himself away, and threw himself into his new marvel working with great enthusiasm.

For the village's part, its citizens went about their lives as they normally did, with Raine's arrival and subsequent self-isolation sending only the faintest ripple through their routines. At times, they even forgot that he had come to the village at all. While they thought him strange on the rare occasions that they remembered to think of him, he was not harming anyone, and he placed no strain on the village.

Until, that is, the day the village woke to find the sea spouting geysers of water. The geysers formed crooked pillars and curving arcs to the sky, agitating the clouds into a frenzy of darkness on the cusp of a storm. When the rain broke, it fell in black and silver sheets into the sea, stirring up mist and froth across the waves.

The villagers beheld this new marvel in horrified awe. Those who were not struck silent began to wonder how they were going to get their boats out to the fishing spots beyond the harbor. A useless worry, as the water remained too rough and dangerous for the boats to venture out at all. Before the villagers could ask one another what they would do for food and how they would trade with the caravans from the inner lands without their bounty from the sea, the water beasts came.

A sharp-eyed boy was the first to see the creatures racing over the waves and around the geysers. Their shapes were strange to him, sleek and elusive like eels but more solid and brawny than any fish he had ever seen. Above the waves, they ran on spindly legs that blurred to fins and flukes whenever they dove beneath the surface. They streamed tails and manes behind them as they burst to the surface and ran across the waves. The beasts were all the color of water, but water at different depths on different days. There, in the front, a deep black beast from the bottom of the ocean. And there, just behind, one of bright turquoise and white foam, the color of sunlight through a breaking summer wave. They ran in a herd of stormy grays, ocean blues, crystal clears and murky depths, completing circuit after circuit around the geysers. The boy spent the better part of a day watching them with his friends, and their watching turned to cheering and then to gambling as they witnessed new winners of each race. They bet shells and marbles and other small oddities, nothing with anything more than sentimental or aesthetic value, but when the boy and his friends returned home with their treasured winnings, they gave their parents an idea of how the village could survive without fishing.

When the traders from the inner lands next arrived at the village, they were surprised to see that there was a distinct lack of fish. In their stead was a terrifying marvel out at sea where beasts of water raced each other along the horizon, a new winner emerging every time. The village had worked hard to scrape together spectator platforms on the beach, and they invited the caravan drivers to sit and watch and enjoy.

And enjoy they did.

So much so that when the village asked the traders to spread the word of their races and help bring people and money to them now that the fish had been properly scared away, the traders agreed without hesitation. And so it went that as the traders went forth and carried goods and the news of the water races, curious people from miles away began to come to see for themselves. The coastal villagers charged a meager admission fee to watch the races, just enough to let them get by on purchases from the caravans. The real money came from the betting pools, where the villagers could draw a portion of the winning pot in exchange for safeguarding the funds and hosting the races.

This went on for the better part of a season, until Raine came into the village to get a new tunic for himself. He felt that, at the very least, the village owed him a new piece of clothing in exchange for the sea-bound beauty he had given them. Not that he would brag about his contribution to their scenery. He had learned his lesson from the last village, and had kept his distance from this marvel, leaving no signature whatsoever in the working. But when he saw what the villagers had done around his hard work, he was shocked, and then angry. He had not drawn up the water spouts for such petty purposes as gambling, nor had he intended for the sea to be ripped up time and time again by the herd of water beasts. He did not know what had attracted the herd nor what compelled them to race across the bay, but he knew it was wrong, all wrong, from the dull crashing of the water beasts over the surf to the roar of the crowds on the beach as their favorites pulled ahead and fell behind. There was laughter and cursing and shouting and screams of delight and disappointment ripping the air apart, and none of the quiet introspection the geysers were supposed to inspire in the villagers.

Sickened by the sight of the villagers profiting off of his work, Raine left the beach as quickly and as silently as he had come, all thoughts of a new tunic forgotten.

The villagers had much to occupy themselves with, now that the geyser races were turning a profit and it was looking more and more like the village would not only be able to survive the winter, but import the supplies needed to fix up several homes before the weather turned bad. All seemed wonderfully well, until the morning the villagers woke to find the geysers gone and the sea calm and silent without any trace of the racing water beasts. The villagers and their visitors spent three days waiting to see if the water would leap into the sky again, but all remained quiet and the visitors needed to return to their lives. They took their money with them, and the villagers gathered to face their options now that their livelihood was, once again, abruptly gone.

Some of them began to wonder if their land was cursed or if they had offended some small god, but the communal pool of profits from the short-lived geyser races proved to be enough to buy and preserve food for the whole village through the winter, and still have enough to patch up some of the worst of the houses. They survived, and when the spring came again, the fish returned to their normal migration routes, and the villagers were able to return to their normal lives. The geyser races became a hazy memory, some fluke of nature that was unlikely to ever happen again, but everyone in that village kept their eye on the sea, secretly hoping that the geysers and the water creatures would return one day. They never did, and eventually were forgotten, just like the abandoned shack on the outskirts of the village that no one ever paid any mind until it collapsed. As the villagers hauled the rotted wood away, they found a broken string of shells burned with strange markings, a few of which had been scribbled out with charcoal. No one knew what to make of the shells, but most agreed that there was something unsettling about them. They returned the shells to the sea and did not speak of them again.

Long before that shack had collapsed and the villagers had found his marvel weaving, Raine had moved inland again. He journeyed far south, into more tropical climates where the sun burned away his dismay and winter could not sink its teeth into his bones. So what if two villages had not been able to understand his marvels? *He* understood and appreciated them. He was sure to find others who did, too. He had just been looking in the wrong places.

So Raine picked a new village to bless with a marvel.

It took some time to find the right one. He needed a place that had no marvel artist of its own, full of people who wouldn't feel the need to bend and warp his creations to suit their own wants. He came upon just the village deep in the forest, one that was isolated most of the year and barely in contact with the traveling traders that passed through. He spent a great deal of time watching them from afar, taking note of their dully colored lives and the rigidity of their routines, and he knew exactly what he wished to create for them.

Raine got to work, spending day after day shaping, collapsing, and rebuilding his new marvel from clay until it was a perfect, delicate sculpture. He blended dyes from plants, and stained the sculpture with wild, beautiful colors and patterns. Then he planted it out in the forest, and watched it grow.

Delicate as the marvel may have been, it was a strong working, and it did not take long for Raine's flowers to take root and blossom. They wove up and down the surrounding trees in a riot of color, catching the light of the sun and exploding across the drab, brown place. Raine spent a few days tending the flowers, but they were growing well on their own and he was satisfied with the working. He put down stones to mark a clear, safe path through the flowers for anyone hoping for a closer look, and then he went to find the villagers.

This time, Raine did not wait for the villagers to discover the marvel, and instead brought them to it. He marched straight into their village, introduced himself, and promised them beauty and wonder if they followed him just a little ways over.

Wary of the stranger promising marvels in exchange for nothing, a few villagers armed themselves and followed Raine. They made certain that he walked ahead of them, and they were careful to only tread in his footsteps, lest they set off some hidden trap of his. But they came through the short journey unscathed, and found themselves gazing in awe.

Flowers in shapes and colors they had never seen before grew along the trees, cloaking them in the beauty and wonder that Raine had promised. The villagers stared, and they smiled, and they breathed in the deep, lustrous fragrance of the flowers. They were happy, and so was Raine.

In the days that followed, the entire village came to see the marvelous flowers. They came in pairs and small groups of family, friends, and lovers, and all stopped to stare at the petals that wove their way over the trees and the ground. They walked among the flowers and sighed happily at the new spirals of colors in their lives, and all was well for a time. Some of the villagers may have frowned a little when they realized how quickly the flowers were spreading, but each new blossom was a new marvel all on its own, and they found that they did not mind the explosive growth much at all.

They still did not mind when they found an old rabbit lying dead among the flowers, its eyes clouded and tongue swollen black in its gaping mouth. Some disease had taken the creature, and the villagers quickly moved the rabbit and burned the carcass before the taint could spread. But in the following days, there were more dead rabbits and a few wild boars among the spreading flowers, and then the birds began to fall from the trees, and the villagers started to worry.

They sought out the young man who had brought these flowers to their home. He'd claimed to have made them, and so he might be able to fix whatever had gone wrong. They found him in the small hut he had built for himself beyond the flowers, situated precisely so the villagers would need to pass through his marvel before they reached his door. Many of them had visited him before to speak of the joy the flowers had brought them, and share a little food with him in thanks. He had always received them graciously. That day, they found him lounging outside, enjoying the warmth of the sun and smiling brightly as they approached.

His smile faded as the villagers described the dead and dying animals and their concerns that the flowers would kill or drive off all of the wildlife, which they needed for food and skins. Something had gone horribly wrong with his beautiful creation, and he needed to come and fix it.

Frowning, Raine explained that there was nothing wrong. The flowers were doing exactly as they were supposed to, and killing the things that tried to eat them. Raine had wanted to give the villagers lasting beauty in their lives; how could it last if it could not defend itself?

The villagers said that the flowers grew quickly, and if the animals ate a few, the flowers would replenish themselves. There were so many now, beautiful but proving dangerous, and the villagers were worried.

Raine smiled at them again, sweet and comforting, and reminded the villagers that his marvel was for them to enjoy, not to fret over. The animals would learn in time not to eat those flowers, and the villagers could go on enjoying them while they waited for the fauna to adjust.

The villagers were uncertain about this, but they did not understand Raine's magic, and so had no choice but to leave him and return home.

Not three days later, one of the flowers bit one of the village scouts on her ankle.

She'd been out with her team, searching for signs that the animals had relocated their nests away from the poisonous flowers, when a rabbit had come leaping out of the underbrush, startling her and sending her stumbling. Her foot skittered into a patch of leaves, and then there was a fast, sharp pain that she thought was a snakebite, but when she yanked her foot free, a blazing blue and red flower clung to her, the petals stiff and burrowed deep into her skin. Her blood turned slow and black in her veins, and she died within the hour, long before her team could get her back to the village and in front of the doctor. After that, most of the village went out to scour the land around them, and they were horrified to learn that the flowers had spread in a perfect ring around their home.

This was not the beauty they had been offered, but a nightmare that had been forced upon them.

So the villagers turned to fire. They burned a path through the flowers, which hissed and snapped and spat venom into the air even as they crackled and died beneath the flames. Three more people died before the villagers could carve a line of ash all the way to the marvel artist's hut. They came armed with torches to defend themselves from the flowers, and cries for help. But when the villagers arrived, they found the hut collapsed, the dust not yet settled, and the artist vanished.

Raine had seen the smoke and heard the villagers coming, and his anger had drowned out the world. How could they burn his gift to them? He had put his heart and soul into his marvel workings, and this was his repayment: destruction of his work; twistings of his intentions; demands that he change it, always change it. He would not. This was his work, and he would not change it. Instead, he smashed the new sculpture he had been working on, and left the shards on the ground before pulling his hut apart and disappearing into the forest.

He knew there were trackers in the village, so he kept to hard ground and then waded through a shallow stream for a ways, destroying his trail. His anger pushed him far, and it wasn't until long after nightfall, when a bad storm had soaked him to the bone, that he stopped walking and huddled beneath a tree, alone and miserable as lightning tore jagged scars across the night.

Raine did not know where else to go. He knew that, no matter where he went, his marvels would be misunderstood, misused, mistaken for terrors. He was trapped in this simple world that would never make room for him, and he needed to escape. But where could he go?

Nowhere, Raine knew, nowhere at all. But as he watched the lightning tear the way open for the roars of the storm's thunder, he realized that perhaps that was not the right question to ask himself. If he was a man ahead of his time, perhaps it was better not to ask where, but when. As a marvel artist, there was nothing he could not do once he had mastered a craft. And lightning could rip the world apart. What *couldn't* Raine do if he tamed the lightning?

So Raine picked himself up and set about teaching himself to dance like lightning, flashing across space in jagged, imprecise, deadly motions. For weeks, he drank little and ate even less, determined to master the marvel and get himself to the when he was born for. His strength waned but he pushed himself on, jumping and darting around the forest, until his motions cracked with thunder. The sound startled the clouds, and they came gathering to answer his challenge. Boiling and racing over the ground, Raine out-danced the storm until, seething over its defeat, the lightning obeyed his call.

Exhausted but triumphant, Raine ordered the lightning to take him to a time when people would appreciate his marvels for the wonders that they were. And the lightning obeyed.

It flashed down around Raine, gathering him up in its energy and shooting them both across time. It came down hard on the same spot, thousands of years away, at just the moment Raine had been hungering for. It left him there, naked and alone. More alone than Raine realized, although he would come to understand his mistake in time. Lightning is a spiteful thing, and taming it comes with a price most marvel artists would never pay.

But even after realizing the true cost of humiliating the lightning and bending it to his will, Raine would blame all those villagers for misunderstanding him, and the lightning for stealing his magic and stranding him in a time that did not have any marvels at all.

Don't Look Back

"Please, just look at me."

My heart jolted at the familiarity of the voice. It touched something in me, something cold and dark that left me scared and shivering. There was something wrong here, but the voice was familiar. Did that mean it was safe? I wanted to turn and find out, but my feet stayed planted and my eyes remained riveted on the flower mere inches away from my nose. So small, so delicate and silken and perfect amid a cluster of ugly, tearing thorns. Many-petalled, yellow with a red center. That meant something. I was sure it did.

"Turn around," the voice begged.

Don't look, the little flower seemed to urge me. *Don't let them take you.*

I could feel the danger around me, tugging at the edges of my brain. There was something here that wanted to devour me. I felt it the way animals feel predators watching them from the dark, poised and waiting for the right moment to pounce and sink their teeth into soft flesh. I was so close to death. I stood on the edge, and I was starting to sway towards that open maw.

I had to resist. For the sake of everyone I loved, I had to resist.

Don't turn away, the flower whispered.

Everything here was wrong, but this little flower reminded me of all the better things that were right. Things like safety. Like protection. Life. Love. Family.

There was something so important about this place. About this room and the thorns.

Why couldn't I remember how I'd gotten here?

"Please," the voice said again. I could hear the promise of tears in the timbre of the words. Everything about that voice was as familiar as a faded memory. I felt the cold brush of fear again, a finger running up my spine. Uninvited. Unwanted. Unsafe.

Wrong.

So very, very wrong.

Something in this room was trying to devour me, and if I could only make myself understand what it was, I would be able to save myself. I knew this with total certainty, though I could not say why. Instinct edged with hope, maybe?

Best not to question it. Only focus on what could help me.

Like a little golden flower shining like a star in the nest of thorns, beauty amid danger. Safety among the horror.

Stay, the flower begged. *Don't turn around. Don't look away. Stay.*

I did not want to leave. I was beginning to remember why I had come here in the first place. A memory took root in my mind, of someone I loved very much dying of a poison most brutal. There was a remedy here, hidden somewhere among the thorns. I only had to survive long enough to find it. So I looked at the flower's beautiful petals, and took strength from its radiant colors. But it was so difficult to ignore the horrible, prowling thing behind me that tried to seduce me with a loved one's voice.

"Please!" the thing scraped again, the voice now raw and wet. "Just turn your head and look at me!" A shadow flickered in the corner of my vision, almost drawing my attention from the flower. Whatever wanted me, it was reaching for me, trying to touch me.

I knew looking at the thing would give it power, but could it still hurt me if I denied it? Could it cut me, make me bleed? Would the scent of my blood feed it, give it strength?

It reached closer, and my body began to turn to defend itself.

Don't, the flower warned, and the red center seemed to pulse like a sympathetic heart.

I smelled something then, woody and sweet and ancient. I took comfort in the scent, but beneath that, there was the smell of decay.

The thing behind me shrieked and retreated. There was another taste in the air now, metallic, I thought, but I could not quite put my finger on it. It was getting harder to breathe. Sharp pain sprouted in my chest, then receded. Had the predator managed to hurt me after all? The pain around my torso felt like claws, and it wasn't just in my chest, but across my back, too.

What had that thing done to me?

I drew a deep breath, hissing through my teeth as the pain tightened, but it brought clarity to my mind. I focused on the flower again with renewed determination. I would survive this, whatever *this* was. I would live. I would find that antidote, get out of this room, run back to my family, never take another breath for granted, do every cliché thing you're supposed to do when you have a near-death experience and get another shot at life.

Maybe I would even take this flower with me. It deserved to be somewhere other than this dark, cold room, surrounded by thorns and the smell of dead things and the ragged cries of whatever was haunting this place. I just knew that I had to get out.

Look at me, the flower said, gold and perfect, offering me a lifeline through the steadily increasing pain.

A scream tore through the air, making me flinch, but I kept my eyes on the flower. The thing in the room with me did not sound intelligent anymore, just garbled cries and sounds. But still familiar.

The sense of danger returned tenfold, shivering up my body. God, it felt like it was physically wrapped around me, so tight I could not move.

You are safe, the flower promised. *Don't turn around. Don't look back. Safe.*

I would not turn around. I promised myself this, and the pain began to fade. A sense of calm washed over me. Warm and soft. I was safe. I knew it. The thing in the room could scream and cry all it wanted. It could tear at me and try to rend my soul. But I would not give in.

My world becomes that beautiful yellow flower with the blood-red heart.

Golden sun and red, red blood.

Something is wrong.

Stay, the flower demands.

Something...

Stay, and be MINE.

All at once, I am ripped apart.

I see things so clearly, then, when the parts of me are no longer a whole.

My sister Natasha kneels behind me. Her bag is thrown carelessly on the stone floor next to us, where it lies open and spills out the medicinal leaves we gathered from this place before I fell into the trap. Natasha is crying and screaming and trying to tear me free of the ropes of thorns that encase my body. There is blood on her hands, running freely down her arms to stain the sleeves of her coat. I do not know if the blood is hers or mine.

A vine lashes at her, cutting across her forehead. It sends her reeling, but she rights herself and returns to me, trying to rip me free. The vines hold me fast, long after I should have fallen. Their spines have torn clean through my heavy clothing to hook into my skin, forcing me to stand before a tangle of thorns that have grown impossibly into the shape of a yawing mouth full of needle-sharp teeth and a writhing bunch of vines that flicker like a tongue.

For one jagged moment, my sister's arm passes in front of my eyes, and I am suddenly aware of the bones on the stone floor around me. I am not the first victim this place has claimed. The realization brings no comfort, for the vines push Natasha away and I can see the flower again, putrid yellow and glowing like an evil eye in the midst of all this darkness and death.

And the flower sees me. And the red center pulses again, hungry.

The last thing I hear is Natasha screaming for me to take my eyes away from the demon flower.

To turn around and look at her.

Please.

Grandmother's Familiar

My grandmother died in autumn, on a golden afternoon marked by changing leaves and departing songbirds. I wasn't there. I found out three days later, when my mother finally called to tell me the news.

"I wasn't going to bother you with it at all," she said, her voice tinny over the phone, "but apparently, you were mentioned in the will, so now we have to make a whole deal out of it."

I had to stop for a moment and give my brain a hard reset. I had been expecting yet another request for money. Since I was seven, I'd been hearing Mom casually mention the worsening state of her bank account in between reminders of all the sacrifices she'd made to raise me by herself, and it had only intensified once I'd been able to legally hold a job. *Not* hearing her clockwork demand disguised for part of my paycheck threw me for a loop. So did the actual news, because I had assumed that Grandma had died a while ago. I had no idea she'd still been alive up until that point, give or take the three days it had taken Mom to get around to telling me. I suspect it took Mom that long because she'd been trying to see if she could finagle the inheritance over to herself instead of me. Grandma hadn't mentioned Mom in her will at all.

Mom had hated her mother for about as long as I could remember. The only reason I'd had any sort of relationship with Grandma was due to Mom's constant need for a babysitter while she bled her early twenties away between two jobs after an ex boyfriend left her with a positive pregnancy test and a note wishing her luck. If she could have afforded someone, *anyone* else, she would have hired out. But Grandma was free, and until I was old enough to be trusted not to set something on fire when left alone, to Grandmother's house I went.

My earliest and haziest memories involve afternoons spent in my grandmother's workshop, standing on a stool and straining on my tiptoes to rest my chin on the wooden table where Grandma ground up herbs and scents to add to the soaps she made. She kept the dangerous stuff up high, and never let me in there when the lye came out, but prep work for the gentler ingredients she'd always let me watch.

I remember the smell of lavender and rosemary and the slant of sunlight through the windows, Grandma's old black cat curled up in a patch of sunshine and watching, always watching, as she ground and molded and set and sang to every bar of soap she made. I remember the quick and deliberate motions of her hands as she swirled oils and sprinkled crushed plants into the batters, and her sly wink as she told me that she was putting magic into the soap. I remember asking if she could teach me how to put magic into things, and the racing thrill of my little heart when she said yes.

I also remember the raw anger in my mother's eyes when I told her that Grandma was training me to be a witch. Mom grabbed my arm, sank her nails into my skin, and snarled at me that magic was not real. It was such a sudden, intense storm of rage that I wet myself in terror. A door slammed shortly after that, and then there was a lot of screaming, both from Mom and Grandma. I cowered on the stairs and cried in the face of all that pain and fury leaking out from behind the closed door, a leak that I had caused with one stupid little surge of imagination.

In the wake of that vocal battle, I still went to Grandma's house. There was no one else to look after me while Mom counted down the days until she could enroll me in school and rely on steady yellow bus transportation and the public education system to soak up a good chunk of my days. So she'd pull into Grandma's driveway in the morning, give me a sharp, hot glare, and order me not to believe a word my grandmother said about magic and witchcraft. When she picked me up hours and hours later, she would drill into me with harsh questions until she was satisfied that I was under no delusions of someday having a bubbling cauldron and a black cat of my own. Terrified of what would happen if I broke open another rage pipe, I said as little to my grandmother as I possibly could in the remaining time I spent at her house. Instead of standing at her side and watching her make soap, I sat on her worn couch and stared at the staticky television and waited for the time to drain away until my mother picked me up again. I don't know if Grandma understood my sudden commitment to the idea that children should be seen and not heard, but she did not try to talk to me or draw me out of my shell. All she did was set me on the couch with a snack and a glass of water while she went into her workshop. A few times, she left the door open in a silent invitation.

I always rejected it.

When Mom finally landed herself a steady job as a corporate secretary on the other side of the country, we packed up and flew away without a goodbye or a backwards glance. If I missed my grandmother, the feeling faded along with the pressuring need to tread carefully between her and Mom lest I break something again. Mom and I were never great, but we were better after we left, and I never, ever intended to go back to Grandma's quiet, sleepy town.

But since I was named in the will and the document stipulated that I had to pick up my inheritance in person, I packed a bag, bought a plane ticket, made a one-night reservation at a motel near Grandma's town, and set off to see what, exactly, the old woman had left me.

I found the whole thing incredibly inconvenient. It was our busy season at work, the weather was getting colder, and I didn't much care to be reconnected with my now-dead ancestor. I also had no fond memories of my early life in that town. It was safe, sure, but it was small, too small to merit even a movie theater. The closest airport was over two hours away, and I had to get a rental car to drive myself along the highway that ribboned its way through the mountains standing between the town and the rest of civilization. It was a pretty drive, with the autumn sun lighting up the changing leaves, but that town…

Claustrophobic.

That was the word for it.

I checked in at the motel a few miles outside of town, dropped off my overnight bag, stretched for a bit, then went to meet the attorney who had my inheritance. His office was almost in the dead center of town, along with the dentist (singular), doctor (again, singular), pharmacy, grocery store, and funeral home. Everything a rural residential population could ever need to live and die in one place, provided they didn't mind being bored out of their skulls while they waited for the dying part.

I was so glad I had moved away.

Grandma's attorney was Mr. Connor, a man who looked like he had been stretched just a bit too far along the vertical axis, with long, thin limbs and a long, narrow face crowned by a thick shock of gray hair. He met me outside of his office. He seemed strangely eager to get me inside, wringing his long, lean hands together and shifting so dramatically from foot to foot that I half expected him to commit the rest of the way to the *Cotton-Eyed Joe* and we'd line dance our way into the building.

"Michelle Blackwood?" he asked as I climbed out of the rental car. At my nod, he sagged with visible relief. "Thank goodness you've arrived. I wasn't sure how much longer we could hold out. It's taken over the conference room and we can't get it back in the cage."

I barely had time to process that bizarre statement before Mr. Connor all but pushed me into the building.

I found myself in a small lobby, a high reception desk to my left and a wooden door to my right. Two people stood as far back from the door as they could, each of them holding what I assumed was the closest thing they could find to a weapon: a mop and a broom. They looked at me as I stumbled in, and their relief was instant and palpable.

"I take it that Mike is still working on containment?" Mr. Connor asked grimly.

The cleaning warriors exchanged a glance, then looked pointedly at the closed door as a shout and a yowl spilled into the lobby.

Mr. Connor winced and informed me that that room was supposed to be soundproof.

"*JUST GET IN THE CAGE!*" someone bellowed from behind the door.

Somehow, I did not think that Mr. Connor had gotten his money's worth on that investment.

A few more minutes ticked past, punctured by more shouting and more yowling. I was almost afraid to ask what, exactly, my grandmother had left me. I was also seriously considering faking a sudden illness and running away from whatever nightmare I had inherited when the door banged open. A short, muscular man stood in the threshold, breathing hard and bleeding from several long scratches on his arms and face. There were spots of blood on his white shirt, and more than a few tears in it. His eyes were wide and angry as they fell on me, and he stalked forward and thrust an animal carrier into my hands before I had time to react. An indignant meow came from the carrier.

"A cat?" I said, dumbfounded. "Grandma left me a cat?"

"If she didn't," the bleeding man spat, "that little hell spawn is yours now."

He pushed his way past me and Mr. Connor, who gave him a stern look.

"Mike, hold on, now," Mr. Connor began, but Mike gave him a look that would have melted steel before storming outside and making a hard left towards the doctor's office. Mr. Connor let him go. "I apologize," he said to me, "but yes. Your grandmother's will stipulates that you are to receive her cat, and you are to have access to her house for one week following her death. I should advise you that we're now on day four of that week."

"Wait," I said. "*Access* to the house? Meaning what, exactly?"

Mr. Connor shrugged his long, thin shoulders. "As I explained to your mother, the will made it clear that you weren't inheriting the property or her possessions. Your grandmother wanted the house and everything inside it sold a week after her passing, with the profits going directly to a local charity. She made all the arrangements herself before she died, and we simply need to see them through. But her will states that you—and only you—are to have access to the house prior to the sale, and that the only thing she was actually leaving you was her cat." He bent at the waist and peered into the carrier at my feline inheritance.

There was a nasty growl before a dark paw shot between the front bars. There wasn't any real danger of the claws catching Mr. Connor, but he shot clear across the room. His two remaining employees leveled their cleaning weapons at the carrier and pressed their mouths into thin lines.

I was back in my rental car less than five minutes later. It seemed an escaped cat threatening to claw everything in an attorney's office to ribbons, including the attorney, was an excellent motivator for having all of the necessary paperwork lined up and ready for signatures. I'd barely finished the last letter of my name when they ripped the paper away and bundled me out the door, wishing me luck and asking me to never bring the cat back there, even if I wanted to renounce my inheritance.

I'd never been much of a pet person, but I did feel a little bad for the cat curled up in the carrier in the passenger seat of the rental car. I still hadn't gotten a good look at it, but I had the impression that it was an all-black cat with yellow eyes. At least, that's what seemed to peer at me through the holes in the side of the carrier as I backed out of the parking spot. I didn't know much about cats, but I could tell that this one was nervous.

Given that its owner had recently died, and then it had been forced into a cage before getting loose in an attorney's office where a muscular man had then tried and eventually succeeded in wrestling it back into said cage, I thought that the animal had every right to be a bit on edge.

I didn't plan on keeping the cat. My apartment building didn't allow pets, and I didn't think I would have much luck flying with an animal. I figured that would be cruel to the cat, too. Nothing like taking an already frightened animal and stuffing it into the cargo hold of a giant machine built to roar across the sky. It would be better to take it to a pet store or a shelter and see if they could coordinate some sort of adoption. I could have set that up ahead of time if I'd known that this was what my inheritance was. As things stood, I had one afternoon to rehome a cat before I had to get a bad night of too little sleep and then catch my flight back home for a big meeting on Monday morning that I could not miss. And Grandma had expected me to *want* to visit her house in between all of that?

"Thanks, Grandma," I grumbled as I turned on to the main road. "What the hell did you expect me to do with a *cat*?"

Grandma, being absent from both the car and life, did not offer a response.

"You can't just dump an animal on someone," I continued. With no one in the car to stop me, I was free to ramble and vent to my heart's content. My heart had a lot on its mind. "I mean, how cracked up do you have to be to leave someone a cat as a surprise inheritance? And with no food or kitty litter or anything to go with it." I glanced at the carrier next to me.

The yellow eyes stared back at me intently.

"I suppose you got your little to-go home there, but I don't think you like it all that much. I mean, *I* wouldn't like it. It's all cold plastic and metal bars, like a prison. The nice attorney probably let you out because he felt bad for you, and then you tried to rip him into a million pieces. So not only did I inherit a surprise cat, I inherited a surprise asshole cat."

The yellow eyes blinked slowly.

"I really didn't need this, you know?" I fumed. "I'm supposed to give a presentation on Monday morning that I haven't had any time to practice because I got called out to the middle of nowhere to pick up an animal I am not going to keep, all because my dead grandmother said I had to on a stupid piece of paper. I mean, what did she expect? Me to take you home with me? Or me to stay out here with you?" I gave an angry huff as I slammed on the turn signal and cruised around the corner. There were no other cars around to witness my courteous road rage. "It had better not be the second one. She didn't even leave me the house! This is even dumber than when she had me believing she was going to train me to be a witch. Like, sure, kids will believe the wildest things, and I *think* I liked her old cat when she babysat me when I was little, but I don't even remember it doing anything except sleeping and watching Grandma make soap. And that's another thing. I haven't seen her since I was nine. She *knew* I lived on the other side of the country. And she must have known *some*one who could take you in." I slapped my hands against the steering wheel. "So why the *hell* did she leave *me* her cat?"

Silence was my answer.

"Maybe Grandma wasn't the cracked one," I said, sighing. "After all, *I'm* the one who's rambling at a cat." I felt very burnt out as the car drifted along. "At least I haven't hit the point where it's starting to respond. I'd have to have myself committed if it started talking back."

"I don't see what the benefit of that would be," the cat said.

I slammed on the breaks and sent the car skidding across the road. We spun in a hard arc over the center lines and off the shoulder, screeching to a halt mere inches away from a tree. I stared at the thick trunk looming beyond the windshield without seeing it. My hands were frozen on the steering wheel, my knuckles white.

"Okay," I said, my voice scratching in my throat. "We're okay. We're fine. We're not dead, we're not in a smoking wreck of a car bent around a tree, and we're *definitely not* imagining talking cats."

"You most certainly are not," the cat said, its voice tinted with disdain. "And I'll thank you not to make yourself dead before we reach the workshop and I have the chance to properly train you."

I did not turn. I figured that if I just kept staring at the tree that I had almost tackled with my car, that would make this weird, stress-induced hallucination fade away. Trees were real, and sturdy, and they did not try to talk to you.

Cats, on the other hand…

"Were you planning on moving this century?" the one next to me asked. "Because they had the cheapest kibble I've ever seen at that attorney's office, and I would very much like to get a proper meal in before we begin your training."

"Just look at the tree," I told myself. "Look at the nice, pretty tree, and wait for the hallucination to pass."

The cat grunted.

I waited, my fingers clenched tight around the wheel, and stared at that tree. I stared so long, a squirrel came out of a hollow in the trunk and chittered inquisitively at my car. Birds started chirping in the branches above me.

I let out a long, slow breath and risked a glance at the cat. It was very interested in watching the squirrel.

I gingerly backed the car up and eased back on to the road. I put the car in drive and gently pressed on the accelerator. Silence settled around me, and some of the tension went out of my shoulders. I would need to seriously examine what kind of whacked out food poisoning I was experiencing that made me hallucinate a talking cat, but I needed to get back to the motel first. Once I did that, I could take a nap, look up local animal shelters, and put this behind me. I exhaled again as I drove on.

"You'd think an attorney would be able to afford better kibble," the cat said.

This time, I managed to stop the car a respectable distance from the nearest tree.

"It's going to be a very long ride to the workshop if you keep stopping like this," the cat said. "And I would very much like to get out of this undignified cage that cheap-kibbled mouse man had his bulldog shove me into."

"The cat is talking to me," I muttered, staring at nothing while the engine idled. I pinched my arm, but there was no dream to wake from. "The cat is talking to me."

"The cat is *trying* to talk to you," the cat snapped, "but *you* are not listening." A black paw poked through the bars at the front of the carrier and swiped in my direction. "Stop flailing like a newborn kitten and make this infernal hunk of metal take us to the workshop."

"*Why* is the cat talking to me?" I was desperate for some sort of answer that would put me back in my right frame of mind. Stress, food poisoning, contaminated air that was in the process of turning me into a zombie, *something* that could explain why reality had just backflipped clear away from me.

The cat made a discontented gurgle and flattened his ears. "The cat is trying to get himself and the witch's heir to the workshop," he growled, "so that the cat may properly train the heir, but the heir has decided to hook her claws into the middle of nowhere and refuses to move."

My stomach performed an uncomfortable feat of acrobatics, and I somehow managed to get the car door open in time to be sick on the pavement instead of myself. I coughed and tried to spit the taste out of my mouth.

"Well," the cat said, "that's not the worst reaction I've ever received. Your great-great-great-great-great grandfather tried to run me through with a pitchfork when we first met. Ended up impaling his own foot. You can imagine why he chose to specialize in healing magic."

I wiped my mouth on my sleeve and rolled back inside the car. My hands were shaking and I felt cold.

"You, I'm not certain about yet," the cat continued. "You weren't around long enough for your magic to fully take root, and now it's been dormant for so long, I can barely smell it at all."

"I don't have magic," I said numbly. "None of this is real."

The cat flicked his tail. "Are we back on that nonsense already? I rather thought you'd worked your way past it after you almost killed yourself with that tree back there."

I looked into the cat's yellow eyes and felt the nausea rise again. I rubbed my arms and choked it back down.

"The kitten can learn." The cat yawned. "Perhaps now the kitten can take us to the workshop."

"I—" The sour taste returned to my mouth. I took a deep gulp of air and looked out the window, at the road, at the sky, at the trees, at anything except the black cat in the carrier next to me. "I don't know what you're talking about," I finally said, rather lamely.

"Of course you do," the cat scoffed. "You used to terrorize the place, always running around making those horrible screeching noises human kittens make, demanding food and the most comfortable spot on the couch with the best blanket. I almost wove a banishing spell on you myself." He made a soft sound that was not entirely unlike a sigh. "But when you watched your grandmother weave her magic, you were captivated, and I knew you had the family's gift in your blood. Magic calls to magic, and I knew that one day you would stop making the screeching sounds and start weaving spells. But then you stopped watching, and not long after that, you stopped coming."

I turned to find the cat watching me intently, pupils large and round against his yellow irises. "Are you talking about when Grandma used to babysit me, and I watched her make soap?"

The cat gave me a slow blink. "Precisely."

"That wasn't *magic*," I snapped, the old terror taking hold in all of the familiar ways, "that was soap and lies and a child's overactive imagination."

The cat hissed. "It was magic of the finest sort, and I'll not have you disrespect your grandmother's craft, or mine."

"Magic isn't real!" I yelled, and then immediately felt ridiculous. Not just because I had yelled at a cat, but because I had yelled at what was becoming harder and harder to deny as a talking cat, and said talking cat's response was to give me the kind of look that could only be described as a smirk.

I was arguing with a magical creature about whether or not magic existed. I was definitely losing.

"Okay." I slumped down in my seat. "Okay, fine. Grandma was a witch and you were her cute talking sidekick and you made magic soap together."

"Familiar," the cat corrected me. "Not 'sidekick' or whatever other undignified label you were planning to bestow upon me." He licked his paw and ran it across his face. "It is a sacred bond between us, and you should not disrespect it."

"Look, whatever weird stuff you and Grandma got up to in her garage is your business, and I try to keep an open mind about this kind of thing, but this is a little too much, and—"

The cat swiped through the bars again. "If you would simply take us to the workshop so we can begin your training, a great many things about your life and your family will come into focus."

Even though he was a good two feet away, I recoiled from the caged cat. "Hold on. You keep talking about training me. Why do you think that's going to happen?"

"Is it not obvious? The bond has been passed, and as your familiar, I am duty bound to assist you with your magic."

"What."

"I'm going to train you, kitten."

"What."

One of the cat's ears flicked back. "The bond, between you and me. Inherited from your grandmother, and all your ancestors before her. Me, duty bound. You, magic. What about this is still unclear?"

"You're not my familiar! You're just a cat that my dead grandmother left to me in her will, and you happen to talk. I'm sure I can find you a nice family that will love that little quirk and not find it creepy *at all*, but I don't do magic, I don't have a familiar, and I *definitely* do not have enough drugs and-or alcohol to accept all of this."

"Well, kitten, I suggest you find some, get yourself into a properly accepting state, and then maybe we can get to the workshop with a little bit of dignity intact, hmm?"

I stared at the cat. "You're encouraging me to get high."

"Or drunk, or both. Whatever gets us out of this wretched machine and into the workshop."

"You would train a drunk witch?"

"It would be far from the first time."

I did not know what to say to that. After a moment, I laughed weakly and said, "Aw, to hell with it. Let's go to the workshop so the talking cat can teach me magic. Maybe I'll include the experience in my presentation on Monday."

The cat grumbled something that sounded a lot like *finally* before curling up inside the carrier.

I paused with my hand on the gear shift. "Hey, what do I call you? Grandma must've had a name for you, but I don't remember what it was."

"Call me whatever is right for you."

"You don't already have a name?"

"Not since your family bound me all those centuries ago."

"I… Oh." I was totally unsure of what the proper etiquette was when speaking with a magical creature your family had enslaved. "I'm sorry. Do you… I mean… Shouldn't I free you?"

The cat leveled me with a flat stare. "Don't you *dare*. Do you have any idea how difficult it is to become a familiar? It took me seven seasons to find a willing animal host, twelve more to find a family who could wield my magic, and another *forty-three* to convince your ancestor to perform the binding ritual. A name is nothing when you can have power and eternity in its place." He stretched inside the carrier before settling into a comfortable loaf. "Although that does not mean you can cheat me out of decent kibble. Eternity is far less pleasant when you are only given the cheap stuff, and I'd rather us not have an unpleasant relationship. Wet food is preferable, of course, but I'm willing to compromise if your finances are on the thin side."

"They're going to be even thinner after all of the therapy I'll need when I get home."

The cat didn't say much as we drove to my grandmother's house, except to correct my sense of direction when I almost took a few wrong turns. Thanks to the magical feline GPS, we made it to the house just before sunset, when everything was painted in dramatic oranges and pinks and the shadows were soft. I parked the car in the driveway and sat there for a minute, staring at the house. In my memory of the place, it was huge, with a sweeping front porch, a towering white exterior, and a thrilling maze inside with nothing but surprises around every corner. Confronted with reality, the memory shattered.

The house was small, sitting somewhere on the "cute" side of real estate terminology. The white paint was worn and peeling, teetering between charming and shabby. The giant front porch of my memory was maybe twenty square feet of screened-in space, and I knew that if I went inside, I would come out on a small, awkward landing between the two floors of the house. I could either go up seven steps to the main floor, or down seven steps to the lower level. I found myself reluctant to do either, but I had come this far. I figured I may as well see what the magical talking cat had in store for me. The worst that could happen was that it tried to get me to summon a demon, but I had seen enough horror movies to know not to draw pentagrams on the floor, or bring a goat within five miles of the property, or do *anything* with candles and mirrors. I was pretty sure I would be fine, all things considered. I was inside the screened porch and had just let the cat out of the carrier when I realized I did not have a key to the house, and the door was locked.

It seemed that in his haste to get me and my new pet out of his office, Mr. Connor had forgotten to take care of that small detail.

I looked down to see the cat sitting next to my foot, watching me expectantly.

"I don't suppose you know any lockpicking spells?" I asked.

"Place your hand on the door and wait for the house," the cat drawled back. "Magic calls to magic, and your grandmother had a strong presence here."

I did as I was told, noting that the cat had not actually denied having any knowledge of breaking and entering, fantastical or otherwise. With my palm pressed flat against the wooden door, I imagined a witch running a magical heist, using spells to charm security cameras and break into bank vaults before flying off into the night with a big bag of money slung over her broom. That, in turn, begged the question of whether or not this cat expected me to take up broom riding in my spare time.

Before I could ask, my hand began to tingle, and then there was a little jolt through my palm. I yelped and yanked my hand off of the door. A faint impression of my hand remained behind, but it faded into the wood as I squinted at it, and then the door swung open.

"Good," the cat said. "I was beginning to think the house was going to reject you." He trotted inside with a flick of his tail, and I reluctantly followed.

Immediately, I was struck by an overwhelming sense of nostalgia braided through with sadness. Things were as I remembered them, down to the color of the carpeting on the stairs and the peek into the kitchen I could get from that awkward little landing if I looked up, but everything was darker and colder and so much smaller than I had expected. I shivered as I put my foot on the half of the staircase that led up to the living areas of the house.

"Not that way, kitten," the cat said. His yellow eyes were watching me from the darkness at the bottom of the staircase. "The workshop is this way."

"It's so cold in here," I said as I followed the cat downstairs. I found a light switch on the wall and flipped it on, relieved to find that the power was still connected. "Feels like the middle of winter." I didn't think early autumn could drain all the heat out of a house like that. It had been a warm day, and the nights weren't that cold already.

The cat was watching me again. "Interesting," he said. "What else do you feel?"

"Aside from freezing?" I tugged my thin cardigan tighter as I looked around. There was the spare bedroom, with its hard, narrow bed and the pink walls and that big wooden decorative key on the shelf that I had thought would take me to a fairy realm if I could find the right door. And there was the bathroom, with the yellow wallpaper and fluffy yellow rugs and toilet cover and that tiny little porcelain sink. And there was the little sitting area with the sliding glass door that led out to the small patch of fenced-in grass that qualified as the back yard, and there was the ancient TV in the corner that only got three channels, and there was the door that led to the garage and that place where I had watched my grandmother make soap. *Magic* soap. I wiped my hand across my eyes and was surprised to find that I was crying.

"I don't know why I'm so sad," I confessed. "I mean, I guess I had some good memories here, but Grandma and I weren't close and…" I took a long, slow look around the lower level. It just felt so small and cold and sad. So, so sad. I wiped a fresh tear away.

"*Very* interesting," the cat said, "and promising." He flicked his tail and headed for the door that opened into the garage. "Come, kitten. I think I know the shape of your magic."

Sniffling and still not sure why I was doing it, I followed the cat into the garage, into Grandma's workshop. I flicked on the lights and gave a soft sigh. This place, at least, was exactly as I had remembered.

It was warmer in the garage than it had been in the house. In the yellow light, I saw the table where Grandma had worked, the wooden bench she had sat on as she ground and mixed scents into lye and oils and poured them into the molds. Over the worktable was the high shelf that held the containers of lye, kept well out of reach of the average child. On the concrete floor were the buckets of solid coconut oil Grandma had driven three hours each way to buy in bulk from the supply shop over the state border. I stepped into the workshop and peered at the jars of dried herbs and color pigments and bottles of scented oils that lined the shelves. I breathed in air that still smelled faintly of flowers and vanilla. The small windows around the garage walls let in little bursts of sunset. I wasn't crying anymore.

The cat leapt up on to a small perch near the work table and considered me for a moment. "You feel better in here."

It wasn't a question, but I nodded anyway.

"That about settles it, then," the cat said. He sat and curled his tail neatly over his feet. "You have spirit magic, just like your grandmother."

I frowned at the cat. "Spirit magic? You mean, like ghosts?"

"Precisely. Your grandmother honed her magic to soothe those who could not pass on after death. I did suspect that would be your specialization too, but I had to let your magic respond to this place without influencing you first." The cat's tail twitched. "I'm glad to see this. Your grandmother's spirit has not been able to move on, and now we can help her."

"Huh?"

The cat sighed. "Your grandmother is still here, kitten, heartbroken, alone, and stuck between life and death. So, if you would," he turned his gaze to the work table, "we're in a position to do something about that."

"What do you mean, she's 'still here'?" I asked. I scraped the heel of my hand against my cheek, wiping away the last traces of my unexplained tears, and something clicked. "Wait, that cold and sadness in the house, are you saying that's *her*?"

"Yes," the cat said. "Now come here."

I did not move, remembering my earlier pledge to avoid anything with even a remote chance of getting me possessed. "You're saying that my grandmother is haunting the house."

"Oh no," the cat said, looking at me sharply. "She had plenty of pain at the end of her life, but she was not a malicious woman. She was a healer, not a haunter, but if we don't give her peace soon, that's going to change. Even the kindest of spirits grow teeth if they are stuck for too long." He crouched down and extended a paw towards the table. "You can help her."

I bit my bottom lip as I gazed at the work station. My heart gave a little leap, and somewhere on the other side of a lifetime, a younger me squirmed with impatient glee and strained towards the table. The older, wiser me held her back. "What if I… don't?"

The cat tilted his head.

"I mean, not that I don't *want* to help her, but what if I can't?"

"You can," the cat said.

"But I don't know the first thing about any of this."

"That's why I'm here."

I held the cat's gaze for a long time. He seemed gentler now. None of his earlier impatience was there. And he looked ready to wait all night for me to start making soap. I did not have all night. I sighed and stepped up to the work table.

Under the cat's watchful eyes, I suited up for soap making. The thick gloves and safety goggles my grandmother had used were still hanging from their respective hooks, and they went on without fuss. I opened the nearby windows and set up the fans to make sure I did not kill myself with the fumes, and then I went to work.

The cat told me to ignore the scents and colors for now, and focus on my intent as we made plain soap. He said that my magic would take hold as I worked, and as long as I held the thought of helping my grandmother in my mind, all would be well. I doubted that, but I tried to think happy, soothing thoughts about her as I followed the cat's instructions on measuring out the water and the lye. He told me very sternly to place that mixture in one of the open windows, and take care not to spill it. When I asked if that was an important part of the magic, he told me no, I would just end up with a nasty chemical burn or blind myself if I wasn't careful. I took a few minutes to calm down after receiving that harrowing bit of information, and then we moved to the oils. Once those were measured and added to a pot, they went on to a hot plate until they were melted down.

At that point, the cat informed me that I could either wait a couple of hours for everything to cool, or he could skip the time for me through his own magic. After a very thorough round of questions, I determined that I did not like the idea of giving a demonic cat permission to blink bits of time out of my life, and we settled in to wait.

I spent maybe ten minutes trying to come up with an appropriate name for the cat, but after a few suggestions, he gave me a disgusted look and asked me if Storm and Graymalkin and Tim were really what felt right to me, and I had to admit that none of them did. He seemed particularly relieved that I had not decided to go with Tim. With my enthusiasm for the name quest dampened, I asked him to tell me some stories about my grandmother and her magic. If I was going to learn magic from a talking cat inherited from my dead witch grandmother, I was going to go all the way.

From the familiar I had yet to name, I learned that my grandmother had always been sensitive to spirits, both friendly and malicious. Childhood had been a bit difficult for her, but her father—the family warlock before her—had taught her from an early age that her magic was not something to be feared, but treasured and kept sharp.

"She learned fast," the cat told me. "Far quicker than most of her predecessors." He paused here to clean his paw and ears. "I suppose she had to. She was more than sensitive to spirits; she attracted them. When the nasty ones came, she had to be able to defend herself. Once she could do that, she wanted to help others do the same."

"With soap?"

The cat shot me a flat stare. "What did I tell you about

disrespecting—"

"I'm not being sarcastic. I just want to make sure I understand everything."

The cat gave me a skeptical once over, then went back to his grooming. "The soap was how she chose to bottle her magic. It was easy to distribute, and harmless if it was lost or stolen. Demon repellant that smells of lavender is not exactly something that moves on the black market."

I snorted. "That's probably way better than what that kind of stuff usually smells like."

The cat looked at me with hooded eyes, and I swore he smiled. "Quite right, kitten."

I pulled my knees against my chest and rested my chin on top of them, my arms wrapped around my shins. "So, is making soap the best way to do this kind of magic?"

"It was the best way for her." The cat turned his head to the workshop table where the soap ingredients were cooling. He seemed almost regretful when he spoke again. "Normally, you would have chosen your own form of spell crafting by now, but you'd been away for so long, I was not sure that even this would work. Your grandmother's magic lingers here, and I hoped it would be able to reawaken your own."

I thought about this for a moment. "Magic calls to magic?"

The cat sat up and curled his tail over his feet again. "Precisely."

"So is that why my magic is the same as my grandmother's?"

The cat tilted his head at me.

I stretched my legs out and leaned back against the work table. "I'm making spirit soap, just like she used to. So clearly I inherited her magic."

The cat jumped over to the work table and sat next to me. "That's not how it works, I'm afraid." His pupils were very thin as he looked at me. "Your grandmother sensed spirits even as a child. You, kitten, did not."

I thought about that for a moment, and did not recall ever coming across any unexplained floating objects or blood-writing on the walls at any point in my life. "I suppose that's true."

"Because it *is* true. Every witch and warlock has their own unique magic. Had you been with us longer, we would have exposed you to different kinds of spell working, and let your magic respond in its own way and time. But…" His pupils expanded, pushing his yellow irises to the edges of his eyes. "You stopped coming, and you were never exposed to other kinds of magic. This is all your magic has ever known, so it took this shape and then went to sleep."

"So… if I'd kept visiting my grandma, I could have learned a different kind of magic?"

"Many kinds," the cat said, "and chosen the one you wanted to specialize in." He flicked his tail and wandered over to the oil mixture. "Unfortunately, it's far too late for that now."

I frowned down at the floor. "So I have to do this, then. I don't have a choice."

"You can choose to do whatever you want with your magic," the cat said, his head over the edge of the pot. "I'm only going to teach you, not control you. But this is the only *kind* of magic you will ever do."

I was surprised by how disappointed I was to hear that. I suppose, when you learn that your grandmother was a witch and you inherited that same kind of power, you want to be able to do all the amazing, fantastic things you used to dream of doing, back when the world was nothing but possibilities. Instead, I was going to make soap that ghosts liked. An unexpected spike of fury shot through me. I could have learned so many amazing, wonderful things if I'd gone back into Grandma's workshop, if I hadn't been so scared of making Mom angry again.

Again.

I sat up with a jolt.

"Mom knew," I said.

The cat froze, even his tail going completely still.

"She knew about all of this." I looked around the workshop, everything bathed in the warm glow of the garage lights, beautiful and familiar and denied to me by my mother's fury. "She didn't want me learning magic."

The tip of the cat's tail twitched. "No," he said. I was surprised by how sorry he sounded. "Your mother…" A shudder ran down his spine. "She could not stand the thought of it."

"Why?" I asked. "This incredible gift runs through our family, and

Grandma wanted to teach me how to use it, but she died and she left you to me just so I could—" I came to a crashing halt as the cat turned his head and looked at me. "Grandma left you to me," I said slowly, "not Mom." I thought I knew why, but the words felt heavy and poisonous in my mouth, and I did not want to speak them.

The cat's whiskers twitched, and he waited.

"Mom doesn't have magic," I finally said, and my chest felt heavy long after the words had left me. My mother did not have magic, but I did, and she had not wanted me to learn how to use it.

My first thought was that she had been trying to protect me, or maybe even herself. A child learning to wield magic surely could have caused no end of trouble. Most children get up to enough of that on their own, even without adding spell-casting into the equation. But I remembered the gentle rhythm of Grandma's hands and the warm, safe feeling of the workshop around me, and I quickly dropped the trust that Mom had protection at the forefront of her mind. The first and only time I'd told her that I was going to learn magic was proof enough she hadn't been thinking about that at all.

People who love you and want to protect you don't scream at you until you're terrified to breathe another word about your own capabilities.

The cat startled me a little when he bumped his head against my hand. I gave him a light scratch under the chin without really thinking about what I was doing, but he seemed to enjoy it. At least, he allowed it to continue for a few seconds before drawing back and saying, "You're getting a bit morose, kitten. That doesn't bode well for what we're trying to do right now."

I frowned at the floor. "Was she jealous of me?"

The cat blinked, but he understood in spite of my non sequitur. "I don't pretend to know why your mother did the things she did," he said. "I only know that she kept you from your heritage, and your grandmother had to die before you could come back to it." The fur on his back stiffened and he hissed. His tail lashed angrily before he shook himself and relaxed his spine again. "I advise you not to push me too far down this path, kitten. I have very few kind things to say about your mother."

"You're not the only one," I murmured.

My mother had made a lot of sacrifices for me, raising me by herself and doing everything she could to keep food in my mouth and clothes on my back, but not once did she ever ask if I was willing to sacrifice *my own magic* for her spite. She'd been taking so much more from me than half of every paycheck I'd ever made throughout my life.

She wouldn't do that to me anymore. She *couldn't*, I realized. Grandma had died and left me her familiar, and now I was back in her workshop learning magic, and it was mine.

"I think I'm going to make some changes when I get back home," I said.

"I think that's an excellent idea, kitten," the cat said, giving my hand another bump with his cheek before sauntering over to the pot of cooling oils. He peered inside and gave a satisfied little grunt. "This is ready," he said. "Shall we continue?"

I nodded and stood up.

Under the cat's careful eye, I combined the two mixtures I'd created and blended them together. I was glad the tools Grandma had used for this were still in their places, otherwise I likely would have had a nasty lye burn up and down my arm. Thankfully, I managed, and the soap batter came together. We skipped the addition of the fragrance, going right into the pouring stage. I went for the tray of individual bar molds, agreeing with the cat's suggestion to keep things simple my first time around.

The moment the first drop hit the mold, the cat began to purr. I hesitated, and the cat gently touched my arm with his paw. "Your magic is waking up, kitten," he said. "I can feel it in the crafting."

I squinted at the soap as I poured it. It was thick and opaque and did not look magical in the least, but there was something about it that drew me closer. The batter had no scent but it seemed undeniably pleasant, and I swore I felt warmth pooling in my heart as the soap pooled in the tray. I wasn't certain that was magic, though. There were no tingling sensations in my hands or hairs standing up on my neck or feelings of boundless power circling through my gut. "Are you sure?" I asked the cat.

"I'm the familiar, remember?" He sat down and gave me another half-amused stare. "Making sure your magic is on track while you learn how to use it is what I do."

"But eventually…?"

"Yes, eventually you will know every last facet of your own magic. For now, trust the talking cat and pour the soap."

I bit back a retort and did as I was told. At the very least, I was enjoying the process. It felt good to make something, even if that something might turn out to be the world's most evil bar of unscented soap.

When the batter was all poured out, the cat bumped my hands away and sniffed at the tray. "Oh, excellent. I can work with this."

He tensed over the tray, as though ready to pounce into the soap, and his eyes began to change color. I had just enough time to imagine wings and horns erupting out of his fur before he opened his mouth in a silent meow, and what looked like a breath on a cold day came out of him at the same moment that his eyes flashed icy blue. Then they were yellow again and the cat licked his chops and stepped away from the tray.

"You can take those out now," he said as he slunk to the edge of the table, still all sleek black feline and not a horn nor cloven hoof in sight. "The magic was strong enough for me to skip the time for the soap by itself. Very well done for your first go, kitten."

In spite of my lingering worries that I was going to accidentally summon a demon, I felt a flush of pleasure at the praise. And if I still doubted that a talking cat was really teaching me magic, I now had solid proof in front of me, in the form of a dozen fully cured, fully dried bars of plain soap.

"Doesn't this usually take a few days?" I asked as I held one up to the garage light.

"Three weeks," the cat said, "but I assumed you would not wish to wait that long."

"You know, I could've really used you when I was interviewing for jobs. Saved me the pain of having to wait for all the rejections."

The cat gave me an exasperated look. "I know I have explained enough by now that you know that would not have worked."

I shrugged and pulled off the gloves and goggles. "Wouldn't have hurt to try." I put the safety equipment away and turned to the cat. "What now?"

"Now, you take a bath."

I froze. "Excuse me?"

The cat blinked. "Take a bath. Use the soap you just made. It will help your grandmother's spirit move on."

"Okay," I said slowly, "I think the room at the motel had a bathtub."

"No, no," the cat said. "You must do it here."

"*Here?!*"

Dry amusement sparked in the cat's eyes. "Is your grandmother's spirit here, or at the motel?"

"Here," I said.

"Correct." The cat jumped down from the table and headed for the door. "The water should still be on in the bathroom upstairs, and there are towels in the linen closet. Let's go."

"This is uncomfortable and creepy," I called after him.

"I know."

One set of pilfered towels and one discussion about personal boundaries later, the cat waited outside the bathroom while I ran the water in the tub. It still felt unbearably cold in this part of the house, and I hated the idea of having to take my clothes off to make my own magic work. I hated that idea for a number of reasons, but the cold was the current contender at the top of the list. I made sure the bath was steaming before I set the world record for fastest transition from fully clothed to in the nude and in the tub, and even the heat of the water wasn't enough to shock the cold from my system. My teeth were chattering and my fingers and toes, while warmer underwater, were reluctant to move. I sank down to my neck, trying to absorb as much of the bath's warmth as I could, and eyed the plain bar of soap I'd placed on the tray next to me.

I was taking a bath in my dead grandmother's freezing house with a bar of magic soap that a talking cat made me make. Easily one of the weirdest days I've ever had.

It wasn't going to get any better if I kept sitting there and let the bath cool. I grabbed the bar of soap and set to scrubbing.

I don't know what I expected, other than some suds and a really unpleasant exit from the bathtub. That was not what happened.

I got the suds, so I knew the soap was serving its practical purpose, but while there were no flashes of light or otherworldly whispers or whatever strange things are supposed to happen in the presence of magic, the air around me grew warmer and lighter. The oppressive sheen of sadness started to lift from the room, and while nothing actually changed, it just looked… clearer. Less blurry around the edges. Like the tears had dried up. And the more I scrubbed, the warmer and lighter and clearer it got. By the time I was finished, I was actually uncomfortable sitting in the hot water, and I quickly rinsed off and grabbed a towel. The air was cool but comfortable on my skin, and I dried and dressed myself without shivering once.

The cat was purring when I opened the bathroom door. "It worked perfectly, kitten," he said. "She's gone."

"So that's it?" I asked. "We're done here?"

"If you wish. Now that your magic is awake and its shape is clear, we are free to explore other forms of crafting and go to other places."

I considered him for a few moments. "You really expect me to be a witch, then? Just stop everything in my life and work magic?"

The cat tilted his gaze up to me. "Only if that's how you want to do it, kitten. If you want to relegate your magic to a weekend hobby or something you only work once a year, you can. If you want to work it every day and lose sleep as you lose yourself in your workings, you can. It's not my place to tell you how you should do it. Only to help you when you need me."

I sighed and glanced around the house. It had seemed so dark and sad when I'd first arrived, and that was with sunlight slanting through the windows. Now, in the night, it was just… there. The sadness was gone, the cold was gone. It was just a house full of things that someone had once owned. Soon enough, someone else would clear it out and put the house on the market, and then it would become a house full of different things owned by someone else entirely. I felt no attachment to it. No nostalgia or longing or even disdain.

It was just a house that my grandmother had lived in.

Where she'd shown me magic.

"Does it always feel like this?" I asked.

The cat gave an inquisitive *mrr*.

"After you do the magic. Does it always just feel like… nothing?"

The cat was quiet for a long time. "I don't know for myself what it feels like," he said, "but I do know that your ancestors found joy in their magic. It wasn't always easy or enjoyable for them, but after it was done… I think a lot of them found purpose, and fulfillment." He blinked at me. "I think you will, too, once you understand what it is that you just did here, and what you could do elsewhere."

"And what if I don't?"

"Then I'll have failed as your familiar," the cat said, "and the bond between us will break, and I will die."

That startled me. "Seriously?"

"No," the cat said. "I'll just encourage you to go see a therapist to talk about what are clearly some very big issues if you're feeling that unfulfilled in your life." He stretched lazily and sauntered towards the stairs.

"You're kind of a dick, you know that?"

"I've been called worse," he said. "Now, I know you have a plane to catch in the morning, and you'll need to eat before the magic drain catches up with your body, so if you're ready, we can be off."

"Lead the way, Dante."

The cat paused and looked back at me. "Dante?"

I shrugged. "I can't shake the feeling that you're going to lead me through Hell at some point."

The cat blinked. "If you decide that you want to use your spirit magic to hunt demons, that would not be inaccurate. But that's your choice. We need never set foot there, if you do not wish." He flicked his tail and slipped down the stairs before sitting and waiting for me at the front door. "Also, the guide's name was Virgil."

"Yeah," I said, somehow unsurprised that the magical talking cat was familiar with classic literature, "but I like Dante better."

"I do, too," the cat said.

I stepped down to the landing and opened the door. Dante trotted out on to the screen porch, and then stepped inside the carrier when I opened it again. He complained about the chilliness of the plastic and demanded that I get him both a blanket and a can of wet food from the pet store, along with a proper takeout meal for myself, but he let me take a moment to look back at the house.

At the place where I learned magic.

Then we left to begin whatever kind of life a witch and her familiar live.

How Not to Make Cookies in Space

There are a lot of things that can wake a starship captain from a sleep cycle. Some of them are soothing, like the ship's A.I. calmly informing you that you've reached the destination system, and it's time to resume your captainly duties. Some are a bit more intense, like the ship's A.I. calmly informing you that you've reached the destination system, but the projected migratory patterns of the metal-eating space locusts were off this year, and it turns out that particular system is now swarming with the things so please get up and choose some new coordinates before the bugs gnaw a hole in the hull. And some are just plain panic-inducing, like the ship's A.I. calmly informing you over the sudden blare of the emergency alarm that there was an explosion in the galley and there is now a climbing risk of asphyxiation if the ensuing fire is not dealt with promptly.

The alarm alone is enough to launch me out of my warm nest of blankets, my heart slamming so high against my ribs that I think it's going to leap out of my throat. Red light flashes in my quarters in time with the pulse of the alarm, giving everything a bloody cast as I scramble into whatever clothing I can find. I learned the hard way that the crew is zero-point-six percent slower to respond to my orders if I present myself to them in the nude, and when giant, void-dwelling insects are turning your ship into a snack, that fraction of a moment can mean the difference between a clean escape and one very harrowing ride through hyperspace with a breached hull. And explosions are an even more immediate threat than hungry insects. So yes, I take the time to tug on a pair of breeches before launching myself out of my quarters.

I fly down the hall and dive into the chute that cuts through the center of the ship, bypassing the curved ramps that normally grant the crew access to their stations. Ladder railings whip past my eyes as I drop three levels to the galley. I come down hard on the floor and know I will be feeling that landing for the next few days, but adrenaline is the ultimate painkiller. I push myself up and soar into the galley.

I am expecting a roaring wall of fire and black smoke. I come up short when I see neither.

Gray smoke is pouring out of one of the ovens, and our single human passenger is frantically waving his hands at the small flames in one of the worst attempts I've ever seen to stop a fire. His eyes are streaming and he is coughing hard as he tries to fight back the heat and the smoke, but this is not the emergency I so willingly got out of bed for.

"Zai," I say, and the ship's A.I. politely pings to let me know that I have her attention. "Why hasn't the fire security system taken care of this yet?"

"I thought you should see this for yourself before I put it out," Zai says in her mellow voice, but I've been with this A.I. long enough to catch the dry spark of amusement in her tone.

"And you needed me awake for this small fire because…?"

"It is standard protocol to alert the captain to all emergencies."

I groan. Zai knows that a small oven fire is not an emergency, even if it was preceded by an explosion. She has another reason for bringing me here, but has decided to be evasive about it. Not for the first time, I regret that I opted for an A.I. with a personality when I bought this ship.

"Please help Mr. Harper before his fire eats all of our air," I say tiredly.

"Of course, Captain," Zai says.

A compartment in the wall slides open, and with a soft *snft*, a pellet of emergency fire foam shoots across the room into the oven. It erupts in a massive wave of white the moment it comes in contact with the flames, smothering the fire, the oven, and Jim Harper in a solid wall of white. The ship's alarm immediately falls silent, and for a moment, everything is very still.

Then Harper sputters and stumbles away from the oven. He

bumps his way along the wall to the sink, leaving a trail of stiff, white foam in his wake.

I flex my wing joints and unplaster my ears from my skull. "What was he doing in here?" I ask Zai as Harper fumbles at the tap and finally manages to get the water on.

"Mr. Harper expressed a desire to bake something," Zai informs me.

"Without involving the cook?"

"He wished to surprise everyone with something he called 'holiday cheer'."

I groan again. "Dust these humans and their holidays."

"We are obligated to allow all crew and passengers to practice their faiths as they see fit," Zai reminds me in her smooth monotone before adding dryly, "although I would advise that we find an acceptable substitute for fire in any future rituals that require it."

"Agreed," I say as I fly over to the oven. I hover for a moment, letting my wingbeats drive a sizeable hole in the white fire foam before latching on to the wall. I dip one of my hands into the oven, scrape away the fire foam, and come out with a black lump. I bring it to my nose and take a cautious sniff.

Past the fire foam residue and the charred crust, I smell sugar, butter, and…

I flip around to look at Harper. "Did you put oolaithe eggs in these?" I ask, making sure my voice is loud enough for him to hear me over the running water.

Harper jerks at the sink, sending a splash of diluted fire foam over the edge. He comes up with his head soaked and water sloshing off of his brown hair, but he's managed to get part of himself cleaned off. Enough, at least, for me to see the embarrassed flush that creeps over his skin. "They were all I could find," he mumbles.

My ears twitch in amusement as I hear heavy slaps echo down the hallway. The cook is on her way, and I'm sure a few other members of the crew are not far behind. Zai will have informed everyone by now that the emergency has been taken care of, but there are some among this crew who need to witness that for themselves before they'll believe it. Like the cook, who was just roused from her own slumber to learn that there was a fire in her domain. She will not be pleased.

"Oolaithe eggs," I say as the incoming audience draws closer, "explode at temperatures above freezing. That is why we keep them *in the freezer.*"

The cook spills into the room at that moment, a shapeless blob of translucent flesh who flops from place to place and has more spirit and good humor than the rest of the galaxy combined. She sloshes to a halt, the three iridescent organs floating inside of her swiveling to focus on the foam-covered ovens. She gives a bubbling sound of mourning, nearly flattens herself against the floor, and then launches herself through the air. I have just enough time to surge away from the wall before she lands, splattering fire foam across the room. Several globs land on me, and I perch on a stool as I wipe myself off. The cook burbles a few phrases that Zai deems too rude to translate, but I understand enough. I decide not to admonish the cook for it; she's too busy fretting over the damage to hear me as it is.

"I believe you owe Shushaash an oven cleaning, Mr. Harper," I say.

Jim Harper shoots me a sour look from the sink. It might have been a more impactful gaze if he wasn't still covered in foam from the chest down, or the one responsible for the need for that foam in the first place.

Two more of the crew arrive shortly after that, bodies tensed and racing with adrenaline: Marinus and Xiaxie, exactly who I expect to come running at the first promise of trouble. My full crew is a motley assembly, pulled from all arms of the galaxy and thrown together into one starship. They're often at odds with each other, making a quiet moment on this ship almost impossible to come by. I wouldn't trade them for anything.

Except maybe a new apprentice mechanic who doesn't feel the need to set fire to the galley, but that may be too much to ask at this point.

I stifle a yawn as I squint at the black lump I pulled from the oven. It is hard in my claws, but the surface flakes and scratches easily. Odd.

"Now that a number of us are present and more awake than any of us want to be," I say, holding the black lump up to the light and watching the fine particles scatter, "could you please explain what the dust you were doing, Mr. Harper?"

It takes a moment for the water to shut off. I hear Harper draw in a deep breath, then the pop of his shoulders as he straightens them. He turns to face us with as much dignity as he can muster. Which is not a lot, given the amount of water and fire foam pooling at his feet. "I was trying," he says, "to make cookies."

Even Sushaash, burrowed deep inside the ruined oven, falls still for a moment.

"The dust are cookies?" I ask, and the rest of the crew murmurs in agreement.

Jim Harper looks at me as though I have doused him with a fresh coating of fire foam. Dismay creeps over his face, and it only intensifies as he turns from me to the cook. She has trained one flashing organ on him, but the rest of her attention is devoted to salvaging her oven. It's clear that no one in the room has the slightest idea what he is talking about.

He sighs and shakes his head, sending droplets of water flying. "No Thanksgiving, no concept of birthdays, and now no cookies." He sloshes over to the table and sinks into the seat next to mine. "Next you'll tell me none of you celebrate New Year's."

"Which one?" Xiaxie asks as she slinks over and claims a seat for herself. She looks at Harper with genuine curiosity as she folds her limbs against her body and settles in, evidently deciding to find this latest sleep cycle interruption charming rather than something that merits removing Harper's head from his body. I find myself grateful for that. "The stellar new year," Xiaxie continues, ticking off each one on her talons, "the first lunar new year, the second lunar new year, the eighth lunar new year, the revolutionary new year, or the—"

"Clearly not one of your frivolous time markers," Marinus spits as he joins us, but there is no real acid in the words. I'm glad he has also decided to be playful, despite the large spear he brought with him to the galley. I frown when I remember that I confiscated that spear from him after the incident with the kitolian merchant, and had not yet given it back. I'll have to ask Zai to remind me to re-encrypt the vault locks.

"We take our annual celebrations quite seriously," Xiaxie says. "Not one of them is frivolous." She pauses. "Well, except maybe the fifth lunar new year, but that is only due to a technicality."

Marinus shakes his great, shaggy head and gives the butt of his spear a tap on the floor. "I told you, humans are closer to us nardute than you fleaths."

"They look nothing like you," Xiaxie returns with a playful snap of her beak. "They are much closer to a fleath than a nardute."

"No offense," Harper chimes in, "but it's pretty clear I'm not like any of you."

"Untrue," Marinus counters. "We both have hair."

"Okay, but mine isn't blue, and does not cover my entire face."

"Do not the adults of your species have chin manes?"

"Some of them," Harper says, "but that's not exactly the missing link between our species."

Xiaxie ruffles her feathers, pleased. "See? He is closer to a fleath."

I drive an amused look up at her. "I know you're excited to have another biped on the ship, but I really don't think his species is all that close to yours, either."

"Nonsense," Xiaxie says. She cranes her neck across the table and gives Harper an affectionate nip on the head, which prompts him to immediately check for blood. "Two legs, two eyes, he is fleath."

"But he doesn't have fluorescent feathers or a beak," I point out, "or stand at three times my height."

Xiaxie takes a moment to peer at Harper through one bright yellow eye. "You are an adolescent, yes?" she asks him.

Harper shrugs noncommittally, still sifting his fingers through his hair as he searches for any scratches from Xiaxie's beak. "I'm fifteen," he says. "Some cultures on Earth considered that a grown man."

That amuses me. "And in your own culture?" I ask.

His skin flushes pink and he says nothing.

"Adolescent," I confirm for Xiaxie.

"Then he could still grow as tall as any fleath," she proclaims.

"I think twice my height is the most our young Harper can aspire to," I say, "provided he gets proper nutrition and does not do unnecessarily dangerous things like *setting the galley on fire*."

Harper's flush deepens to red and he takes a sudden, intense interest in the surface of the table.

"So he would be a tall nardute," Marinus says smugly, "*and* he would celebrate a single new year, *and* another year of survival, just as we do."

Harper gives him a pained smile. "No offense, but having the entire neighborhood scale a cliff and then chuck rocks over the edge isn't the same thing as stuffing yourself with sugar and celebrating the day you were born."

"This is what you do to celebrate the passing of a year?" Marinus asks.

"On your birthday, yeah."

"I thought that was the day you were given free things from other humans?"

"Well, it's one of those days."

"Well," Marinus says, thumping his spear on the ground again, "at the celebration last year, I got this spear from one of my war wives, and *he* got a shield from one of his wives."

Harper scrubs his hand over his face. "Marinus, once more, 'wife' does not mean what you think it means."

Marnius scrunches his furry face in confusion. "Life partner, no?"

"Well, yes, but…" He gives up and slumps back in his seat, looking to me for help.

My lip curls.

"Captain," Harper says, "are you laughing or snarling?"

"A bit of both at this point," I reply. "I warned you that being the only human on a back-system freighter would be difficult for you, but you need to remember that you're not the only one isolated from the rest of his species."

"I know," Harper says, and I can hear the apology in his voice. "I'm trying to get used to things, really. It's just all so different from what my life on Earth was like." He frowns down at the table again. "There's a lot I still need to learn."

I tilt my head and consider Harper, picking up the familiar rawness that underscores the word "Earth" every time he says it. I think I am beginning to see the real reason why Zai wanted me awake.

Sushaash burbles from the oven, and whips a tendril of herself over to slap the table in front of Harper, making him jump. She drums out a short rhythm on the table, staccato and pointed. Harper watches her blankly.

"Learning how to avoid destroying the ship with attempts at confectionary would be a good place to start," Zai translates for him.

The flush returns. "I am sorry about that." He swivels in his seat to address the cook. "I mean it."

Sushaash extends herself once again and gives Harper a light pat on the head before returning to the oven and sloughing out the rest of the fire foam.

A heavy wave of sadness runs over Harper as he settles back into his seat, strong enough for me to smell it as it envelops him. I understand now. Zai was right to wake me up.

I clear my throat and place the charred lump from the oven on the table, giving it a light tap with my claw. "In the spirit of understanding each other a bit better," I say, "why don't you tell us what you were attempting to accomplish with…" I gesture at the lump.

Harper chuckles weakly. "I got it in my head that I'd surprise everyone with cookies. I guess the surprise part was a success. The cookie part, not so much." He looks up and sees us watching him, interested but still confused. "Oh, um, cookies are this sweet food from Earth. There's a lot of different kinds of them, but every year, back on Earth, there was this holiday called Christmas that my family celebrated. Uh, family is like clanmates," he says, nodding to Xiaxie. "So we'd all get together, and we'd exchange gifts and eat special food and just… have a nice time, even if we had to pretend sometimes." He gets a far-off smile. "For the party, my mother used to bake a huge batch of cookies every year, and I always helped. She let me decorate with the icing and I always had so much fun with that. One year, we made so many cookies, we were still eating reindeer and Santa hats on Valentine's Day. They were so stale but it was tradition that we never throw out the Christmas cookies, because it would bring bad luck to Santa Claus the next year."

We allow Harper a quiet moment of reminiscence and reflection, but as he comes out of it, a glance around the table reminds him that he has just used a lot of words that none of us understand, and he is going to regret that for the next several minutes.

Marinus strikes first. "I am confused as to why you were eating hats and deer of rain if the Earth cookies were so important," he says. "Unless the cookies were used to lure in the bigger prey so you could feast upon them?"

"No, they—"

"What is Vale and Time's Day?" Xiaxie cuts in. "Is that like the third lunar new year?"

"Valentine's Day is a holiday that—"

"Acht, how many holidays do you humans have?" Marinus asks, his bluntless due far more to a lack of tact than a desire to offend, but I'm inclined to agree with him.

I've worked hard to familiarize myself with each crew member's individual religious and social customs, but Jim Harper the human has proven to be a special challenge. When the refugee program matched us with the young aspiring mechanic from Earth, I went through a database of all human holidays with Zai so we could be prepared. I'm familiar with the concept of a single species having more than one religion, but I never expected so many religious *and* cultural variances across territories, let alone within individual *families*. And that was just the information that had survived to be catalogued. Suffice to say, even the A.I. was spinning with confusion when we finally gave up.

"Look," Harper says, trying to steer the conversation back on course. "The point is, I wanted to make cookies since they were something I thought everyone could enjoy. I know everyone in the crew likes sweet things, and I wanted to make it a nice surprise, since you all took me in after…"

Yes, after.

Another silence falls, this one heavy.

The destruction of Earth had very different impacts on all of us. Until the planet sent out its distress calls, most species had never even heard of it. My fleath and nardute crew members were living proof of that. The rest of us had at least a vague sense of Earth's existence prior to the disaster, and we understood what it meant for that planet to suddenly stop existing. By the time the refugee program matched us with Harper, he was part of an endangered species.

That must be hard for him, but he does not like to talk about it. I know he was part of a family once, with parents and a younger sibling, but they perished with the planet while Harper had been away at the lunar colony school. That small grace had given him an extra twenty minutes to evacuate before the moon followed the same destiny as its planet. Those minutes had made all the difference; Harper and a handful of other humans had survived. The rest had not.

Most of the survivors chose to stay close to the remaining humans. Those were the people who had others they could turn to. From what I gathered from Harper's history, he had been awarded a scholarship to the lunar school, a mid-semester transfer that had been a blessing, but had also uprooted him. He had just begun to settle in and meet his peers, most of whom had been born on the moon and had their families with them. Then his planet blew up and the people in charge threw him on a ship and out into space.

I think he pretends that if he keeps moving farther and farther away from the hole where his home used to be, he won't have to admit that it's gone. I'm certain that's part of the reason he signed up for the matching program and took the posting as an apprentice mechanic with us. That was almost a year ago.

In his early days on the ship, he cried a lot during the sleep cycles when he thought no one could hear him, and Zai reported that he often looked at a holopic of his family. He still looks at the holopic, but he cries less. I'm waiting for the day he understands that it's safe for him to open up to anyone on this crew. We all know the sting of loss. We also know that, sometimes, you need space wherever you can grab it. Zai keeps silent watch over Harper, making sure his grief does not turn harmful to himself or others, but I've asked her to give him privacy as much as she can.

When he's out with the rest of the crew, we try not to linger on the past.

"You're one of us now, Harper," I say, resting a gentle claw on his shoulder. I make certain not to grip him too tightly, and he relaxes after a moment. "And it was a lovely thought to try to surprise us, but maybe next time, ask Shushaash before you start picking out your ingredients."

He quirks a sideways smile at me. "I think I've had enough surprises for one lifetime."

I pat his shoulder, glad that he is able to move past his own mistake so easily. I wish he had come to us under better circumstances, but he has a quick mind and a good character and a bright future before him. We can help him reach it, if he'll let us. No harm in encouraging him a little.

I glance over my wing at Shushaash. She senses my gaze and

swivels an organ around to watch me as I tilt my head and gesture questioningly at the scorched food on the table. The cook's organ flashes purple in acknowledgement, and she immediately sets to work. I rejoin the conversation at the table just as Xiaxie offers Harper some culinary advice.

"Next time," the fleath says, "when you use oolaithe eggs, mix everything in a large bowl inside the freezer. It will be cool and pleasing, and we can carve lumps off whenever we want a piece. Good for sharpening claws *and* for sweet treats!"

"No, no, no," Marinus says. "You must forget the eggs entirely, and eat the butter raw with the sugar as a garnish." He smacks his lips and thumps his spear again. "That is a *much* faster way to add weight to your frame."

"That's not… really the point," Harper says.

"Do you not consume the cookies in preparation for battle with the clawed Santa creature?"

"No, but, now that you've said that, I think you probably would want to bulk up if you were going to take on Santa. That guy works with reindeer and deadlifts a giant sack of presents. He definitely knows how to wrestle."

"About these deer of rain," Marinus begins, but he is interrupted by Shushaash plunking down a tray of intricate shapes brightly coated with thin swirls of color. A sweet, pleasant smell drifts up from the tray, and everyone around the table perks up with interest. I nod my approval at the cook, and she burbles happily.

Harper picks up one of the shapes and cradles it in his hands as though it is a holy relic.

"Are these *cookies*?" he asks.

Shushaash slaps a response on the table. Zai translates it to an affirmative.

"But we've only been sitting here for a few minutes," Harper says, throwing an incredulous look at the ruined oven. "How did you make these so fast?"

Zai's translations inform us that Shushaash rounded up a few substitutions to make a sweet dough, which she then cut and wove into the complex shapes. Then Shushaash flash heated them herself before liquifying the remaining sugar and pumping the colors into it for the frosting. The whole process took her less than two minutes.

Harper is still and silent for a long, long time. Then he starts laughing. "That's not how you make cookies," he says, then shoves the one in his hands into his mouth. His eyes go wide as he chews and swallows, and then he is smiling and reaching for another one. "But these are the best damn things I've tasted all year."

"Perhaps do not say things like that to the person who has cooked all the other things you have eaten this year," I advise Harper.

But as the crew laughs and we all dig in to the treats, I find that I'm inclined to agree.

About the Author

K.N. Salustro is a science fiction and fantasy writer who loves outer space, dragons, and good stories. When not at her day job, she runs an Etsy shop as a plush artist and makes art for her Redbubble shop, both under DragonsByKris. She was serious about loving dragons.

For updates, new content, and other news, visit www.knsalustro.com.